Dyslexia Fri

Written By a Bridgwater Man

The story of Hope

A once in a lifetime adventure full of loss, sadness, love and friendship. Full of hope.

How generations come together in search of treasure.

When you think all is lost, then all you have left is hope.

Scan the QR code on the back cover to check out the story

Richard Bell

Search the Story of Hope on Facebook.

THIS HAS BEEN WRITEN BY A DYSLEXIC MIDDLE AGED MAN WHO HAS NEVER READ A BOOK.

Acknowledgments

You're all amazing people

Vicky who helped kick start the story with her amazing positivity and encouragement.

Sharon for being the first person to read the draft copy and encouraging me to keep going.

Sarah S who committed her time, patience and walked the journey with me. Supporting me, mentoring me, questioning me, telling me the truth and being so honest. Some people in the world are just beautiful people and I'm so lucky to know this one. Thank you, Sarah, for being with me from start to finish. This book would not have happened if it wasn't for you. I remember when we had a book meeting on a warm summer's day in our local cemetery, talking through the plot and the characters. You just got it and understood my struggles. Your enthusiasm inspired me to keep going.

My Wonderful, very patient and understanding wife. You never doubted me and always encourage me. I know you lost me to this journey for a while but thank you for always being on hand when I needed you. You supported me with spellings and all that lovely stuff that goes into writing a book. You were always there for me.

My amazing Daughter who sat with me for hours, checking punctuation and spelling and for making sense of big chunks of word vomiting. There were times were we both laughed and cried together. You are truly very patient and understanding. Hours and hours spent drinking tea in front of the fire watching me meltdown about the word 'outnumbered,' you never stopped encouraging me.

Ian for giving up your time to read it and for being so honest and supportive with your wise words as always.

Julia C for being just an amazing inspiration, writing your own book at the same time and sharing your experiences and encouraging me along the journey.

Contents

Prologue: Nature's way   1

Chapter 1:   The box   5

Chapter 2:   It's out there   9

Chapter 3:   Is she the most beautiful
              person in the world?   13

Chapter 4:   Words of wisdom   17

Chapter 5:   Sink or swim   25

Chapter 6:   Drifting between dreams and reality   33

Chapter 7:   Swimming lessons   43

Chapter 8:   Opening up   51

Chapter 9:   The truth   61

Chapter 10:   The box, the map and the boat   69

Chapter 11:   Recruitment begins   81

Chapter 12:   Preparation is key   89

Chapter 13:   Dive day   99

Chapter 14:   We dive again   111

Chapter 15:   The realisation   115

Chapter 16:   The negotiation   125

Chapter 17:	The meeting	137
Chapter 18:	Behind the red curtain	149
Chapter 19:	The smell	159
Chapter 20:	Random acts of kindness	169
Chapter 21:	I will	179

Life's complicated the alterative ending

Chapter 1:	Safe	197
Chapter 2:	Questions and confessions	203
Chapter 3:	Keys	211
Chapter 4:	Reunited	227

About the Author   255

Prologue

Nature's way

October 1789.

As the day slipped away, La Esperanza found itself falling deeper into what could only be described as impending doom. A ship carrying precious cargo from the distant shores of Spain, was now caught in a mighty storm gathering on the South East coast of Cornwall. The captain of this fine vessel stood tall and proud at the bow of the ship, only to disguise the fear that engulfed him as he knew what was coming. He could see in the distance the darkness crawling towards them. His weathered and wrinkled hand reached out to a large bell raising the alarm, the sound was haunting. Rain lashed down with relentless fury, blurring the lines between sea and sky. Knowing the perils that the Cornish coast presented, but with no other choice the captain was forced to seek refuge.

Twilight descended upon the craggy cliffs and turbulent waters, the crew of La Esperanza battled desperately against the forces of nature. The wind whipped through the rigging, sending icy shivers down the spine of every sailor on board. Mighty waves smashed into the ship, the decking transformed into a slippery, perilous surface where brave men struggled to keep their footing. The ominous darkness clung to the ship like a deathly cloak. Lightning cracked across the sky, momentarily revealing the deepest terror etched on the crew's drenched faces. Amongst the chaos only the captain's voice could be heard, a deep bellowing sound as if it was part of the storm itself. The ship creaked and groaned under the immense pressure, its timbers crying out in agony as if sharing the anguish of its doomed crew. The sails flapped wildly in the relentless gale. Horror and dread hung heavy in the air, an oppressive fog clinging to the hearts of every sailor. They knew their fate was sealed, that the icy waters of the English Channel would be their grave.

In the final heart-wrenching moments, as La Esperanza surrendered to nature's way, the ship is driven towards jagged rocks of the shore. With a thunderous crash, the ship's hull splintered. The crew's cries and prayers were drowned out by the deafening roar of the storm, lives extinguished in a cruel and unforgiving dance of death. The South East coast of Cornwall is swallowed by darkness. La Esperanza, once a proud vessel, now twisted, gnarled, and battered. Nature, powerful and unforgiving, claimed its victory. No one survived that night; the crew and cargo were lost to the bottom of the sea.

Chapter 1

The box

Days pass by, and sunlight dances upon the surface of the water once again. Calm restored and gentle waves whisper secrets to the shoreline, where signs of the shipwreck are present. Two local fishermen, and old friends, set out towards their normal spot in their small, weathered boat. Tristan Richards' gnarled hands grip the oars with familiarity, whilst William Thomas' face displays the same wise gaze over the waters they have been rowing for years. The timbers and remains of La Esperanza lie scattered between rocks and inlets, creating an eerie display.

William and Tristan are silent as they row, honouring the lives lost in the recent storm - lives of fellow seafarers. In the distance seabirds circle above in a sinister, ghostly pattern.

The two friends exchange glances, their curiosity piqued by the remnants. They find themselves drawn ever deeper into the ship's remains. A deafening silence hangs over the scene, accompanied by a smell not recognizable. The bodies of the ship's crew floating, some bloated and disfigured. The birds have begun to dismantle their remains, nature having a crude way of recycling; even the dead are not wasted. You'll never forget the sight of a bird pecking at a dead man's face.

"Whadee reckon?" William asks, squinting at the wreckage, fearful he's seeing a true curse of fate. Tristan, whilst scanning the horizon responds with a tainted tone, "I reckon she'd bee Spanish. She met quite a fate in tha' storm, 'ave a look for any life." The small boat weaves its way through the debris. Planks that once formed the ship's hull are now broken and splintered. Once a proud vessel now destroyed, a testament to the power of nature and the fragility of human life.

"William!" shouts Tristan pointing towards some remains. "Therr, do ee see?"

A glint of something precious among the destruction. Wedged precariously between two large, shattered planks is a delicately carved box with Spanish words etched within its dark-stained wood. William catches sight of jewels and golden bars still within the box.

"Get I closer," demands William. Tristan weaves the boat through debris whilst pushing wood out of the way with the oars, aligning alongside and within reach of the box. With steady hands, William reaches out towards it. Suddenly, the planks part and a wild splash of murky water soars – *kerplunk*. The contents of the box falls into the dark depths, slowly disappearing from sight.

Without a thought, William scrambles out of the boat and with a gulp of air, dives down into the icy cold water. Grasping for the box before it finds its final resting place, he finally manages to latch onto it. His blurred vision fixated on the light bouncing off the precious jewels falling into the deep. As he grabs hold of the box, he notices some jewels remain inside. Quickly gathering up the remaining treasure, William shoves it into his pocket and out of sight before returning to the surface. The fisherman, breathless, hoists himself back onto the boat with the help of his old friend. The dark-stained box lay empty.

Tristan eagerly asks, "Did ee get tha' treasure?"

Unable to meet Tristan's eyes William replies, "nah, twas too late. Tis gone."

William doesn't reveal his findings to Tristan, not wanting to share the wealth he was so lucky to had found. Tristan has his suspicions, doubting that William has been honest, over time distance grows between them and their friendship was never to be the same again.

Chapter 2.

It's out there

May 2012

The sun hangs low in the sky, casting a warm golden hue over the calm and tranquil sea. Cornwall could be the most beautiful place in the world. A father and his young son sit side by side on a weathered wooden bench, their faces lit by the soft light.

"Out there, Son, lies a story as old as time itself. A legend of a Spanish ship called La Esperanza, which I believe means The Hope, sank to the bottom of the sea in a terrible storm." The rhythmic sound of gentle waves lapping against the shore provides a soothing backdrop as the father begins telling the story. The young boy's eyes are wide with intrigue as he leans in closer to his father.

"Legend has it," the father continues, his voice brimming with excitement, "The Hope was no ordinary ship. It's said she was full of treasure; gold, silver, and precious gemstones." The young boy's imagination soars as he visualises the grandeur of an amazing Spanish galleon.

"The mighty storm battered the ship. The waves grew tall, and the winds howled." The boy's eyes remain fixed out to sea, the father goes on. "The Hope met its end son. This was to be her final day." The boy can't help but shiver at the thought of such a dramatic and tragic tale.

The fathers voice now filled with a mix of wonder and awe, "But here's the most magical part. Every so often, when the sea is calm and the moon is just right, you can glimpse the ghostly outline of The Hope beneath the waves. On those nights, the treasure still glimmers, waiting to be discovered by anyone brave enough to seek it." The young boy's eyes sparkle with a sense of adventure, his heart now captivated.

"I think I can see it Dad! It's there!" He points out into the distance.

"One day son. One day, that treasure will be ours."

Not even a week later, my world changed forever.

*

I was only nine as I sat there that day with my Dad, fantasising over lost treasure. My Dad was my hero; a kind, caring, fun man. We spent all our time together wandering the coastline, beachcombing and going on adventures. I loved him so much.

When I arrived home from school that day in May, something felt different. The house seemed to hold its breath, anticipating something yet unspoken. I kicked off my school shoes and helped myself to a biscuit from the tin. No sign of Mum or Dad, where was everyone? As I peeked around the living room door, I noticed Grandad sitting in our armchair, his face weathered with lines of wisdom yet sorrow. "Son." Grandads arms trembled as he reached out towards me.

"There's summat I need to tell yew son," his voice was quivering.

Scared, sensing something wasn't right, I whispered, "What's up Grandad?"

His eyes glistened with tears as he struggled to find the right words. "Son, I wish therr was an easier way to say this. Yer Dad's been in a diving accident. Ee's no longer with us."

The words echoed within me as if they were carving pain into my very soul. A mixture of dizzying confusion and disbelief ran through me, leaving me breathless and feeling sick.

"Daddy ain't coming 'ome son." Grandad pulled me into his embrace and held me tightly. I cried so hard it was painful. I felt Grandad's heart beating as I clutched him tight, no one and nothing could've prepared me. I felt empty, numb. That night I laid awake feeling so alone, the thought of never seeing my Dad again, never hearing his voice was unbearable. Grandads words, *Daddy ain't coming home*, replayed in my mind over and over, Grandads face covered in sorrow was the last thing I saw as I slipped into sleep. Why's it so painful when you lose someone? How are you meant to cope?

Chapter 3

Is she the most beautiful person in the world?

March 2024

Stood on the beach, the sand's warm on the soles of my feet, and the gentle breeze from the ocean has a familiar touch. How lucky I am that Cornwall is my home, it's truly beautiful. Over the years I've learnt how important it is to be in the moment. So often, our minds like to be in the past or in the future - neither really exists. It's the present that really matters, being in the moment is everything. Feeling the wind, tasting the air, being kissed by the sun - never take moments for granted, you'll find happiness there.

I find myself utterly entranced, just gazing. Mesmerised. I'm currently staring, captivated and unable to look away from the most stunning girl I've ever seen. She has a group of young enthusiastic surfers bouncing around her, keen to learn. She stands tall, with beautiful posture. Her long dark hair cascades down her back and her skin has a warm, sun-kissed glow. Her presence seems to cast a gentle spell upon me, everything else is insignificant. You feel it deep within when you see beauty with your own eyes. Her smile, when it graces her lips, is like the first ray of sunlight. Gushy, I know, but she's lush ... proper lush. I think I'm in love. I can hear Bob Marley's "Is this Love" playing out of Sam's café, confirming why my hands and feet are so sweaty and why butterflies with big boots on are stomping around inside my stomach. You know that overwhelming feeling of vulnerability you can't understand or even make sense of? A rush of outta control emotions, this is exactly how I'm feeling. Sick with love.

Her name's Alice. She's new to the area and stands out. Not just because she's so bloody beautiful, but because we live in a small coastal haven. I've grown up here, tucked away from the world and where everyone knows everyone. Unlike a large town or city where individuals blur and blend into the urban spool of noise and activity, everyone stands out here. Everyone's noticed, no hiding in a coastal Cornish fishing village. That's what I love so much about small communities, everyone matters, and nobody can blend in or disappear. Alice is our new surfing and diving instructor. Have I mentioned she's beautiful?

Sam is one of my dearest friends and he notices that I'm fixated in one direction, glued to the sand, unable to move. Realising what's at the end of my fixed stare, he shouts over to me, "Tim! Tim!" louder each time, hoping to break me free from my trance. I snap myself out of said trance and make my way over to Sam's café, occasionally looking back over my shoulder to check she's real and still there.

Sam's café is an extension of the natural environment. A quirky hut constructed of driftwood with faded rusty signs swinging, advertising the delights within: Cornish pasties, locally made ice cream, jacket potato's, cream teas (jam first, of course), and probably the best hot chocolate in the world. His uncle owns it, but Sam's in charge and runs it on a day-to-day basis. The vibe is cool, a constant hub of activity. Outside, locals and tourists gather together on wooden benches under a weather-beaten canopy. The sand and sea, in all their glory, are right there in front of you.

"You're gunna have to talk to her one-day Tim. If she notices you staring at her every day, she'll think you're a right weirdo, and that's gunna ruin any chance of getting to know her. Just talk to her dude."

Sam's a vibrant young man, brimming with an infectious energy and he has a very mischievous grin. His hair's short, a simple buzz cut, and his eyes are a warm hazel, sparkling with an ever-present glint of humour and light-heartedness. Sam's cool, a social creature who finds it easy to talk and get along with everyone. Those who are blessed to know Sam, absolutely adore him. He's fun, a little childlike and always up for a good laugh. He played an important part when I lost Dad; he always sees the positives in life which helped me through some of my darker days.

Daisy walks over, and hands me a hot chocolate with a mountain of cream on top. "Here you go weirdo." Daisy is Sam's girlfriend; they've been together forever and share the same degree of energy and humour. Together they are a right pair, they work hard but play harder.

"You coming Friday Tim?" Daisy asks. I look at her blankly. "Friday? What's happening Friday?" I've never been good at keeping track of what's happening after tomorrow. It's all that living in the moment stuff; sometimes I forget there's a tomorrow.

"The gathering," she replies. "The surf schools holding their annual gathering at Bottom Beach." Sam jumps in, "She'll be there Tim, Alice, she'll be there man. You need to grow a pair and talk to her dude." Both Sam and Daisy giggle as if they're children again. "The normal crew will be there, plenty of people staring into space man. You'll fit right in, at least she won't notice you staring at her all night; she'll just think you're a stoner." Sam ruffles my hair aggressively and walks off sniggering, which quickly turns into laughter.

Almost simultaneously, two conflicting streams of thought wash over me. She'll be there: a moment of excitement. Oh my God, she'll be there: a moment of overwhelming apprehension. Perhaps Sam's right. I just need to grow a pair, I just need to be brave and have the confidence to talk to her. Confidence is a strange thing and something I've always struggled with.

Chapter 4

Words of wisdom

After losing Dad, any confidence I had was stripped away, stolen from me. Not long after Dad died, doctors arranged for me to meet with a therapist. I can remember thinking that was the last thing I wanted to do. I hated the thought of it. It made me feel different, and at that moment in time, all I wanted was to feel normal.

My therapist was called Mrs Appleton, a large black lady with a deep, rich Jamaican accent. The first day I met her, she stood towering over me, dressed in bright colours. She said, "Son, mi hear yuh lose yuh Daddy, Come, child," she grabbed hold of me and pulled me into her, giving me the biggest squeeze ever. I can remember feeling so safe in her embrace. I think that was all I really needed to be honest; just a big cuddle. She loved biscuits. We used to sit eating packets of them, just talking mostly rubbish, but we used to laugh a lot. One day, I asked her about confidence and her response has stayed with me all this time.

"To be truly confident, mi child," she declared, "ya

haffi know yuh strengths, weaknesses, values, an' wa yuh aim to achieve. Yuh haffi able to bounce back from dem setbacks, failures, or criticism. Confident people dem, dem look pon challenges as chances to learn an' grow an' develop. You nuh need confidence, mi child, yuh just to be yuhself. Jah seh yuh already have di confidence, just' believe inna yuhself always."

"Now, yuh must listen to me Son. This hatin' yuh doin' to yuhself, it haffi stop. Yuh Daddy's death nah your fault, yuh nuh cause it. Don't yuh realise how precious yuh are, yuh haffi recognise dat?" Mrs Appleton continued, "If yuh found an animal or creature so special, unique, a true miracle, and I ask yuh to look after it, would yuh?"

"Of course, I would, Mrs Appleton."

"Would yuh treat it right, wid kindness, love it an' never hurt it?" she asked.

"Yes, obviously I would."

"Well, Son, dat's you. Yuh are dat special, unique ting. There nah another you inna di whole wide world. Yuh haffi realise how special an' beautiful yuh are, an' start to look after yuhself wit' dat same amount of care an' dedication. Yuh understand how important yuh are, Son? Only den yuh can find true love, peace, an' dat confidence yuh searchin' for, yuh know?"

I sat and just listened to her voice. It all made such sense. Right then, in that session, I decided to learn to love and respect myself. It's truly strange how one person can have such a profound impact on your life. I swore Mrs Appleton was an angel.

After Dad's death, Mum worked every hour to help keep the house together. I now understand that it was her way of coping - just keeping herself busy. I once felt anger towards her for never talking to me about it all, but now I know she also had to learn how to cope in her own way. Nan also left Grandad shortly after Dad died and moved away. This was a real shock to us all, and I remember feeling so sad. Losing Dad was one thing, but Nan leaving seemed unbearable at the time. I can remember feeling completely abandoned and, for some reason, blaming myself. We still get cards at Christmas from Nan, but that's the only real contact we've had for years. Mum said Nan couldn't handle the loss and had a breakdown - too many memories, she needed a fresh start. I never fully understood that. Why try to leave your memories? Surely memories follow you wherever you go! Not long after Nan left, Grandad moved in with us, much to Mum's despair, as he brought a 19-foot boat with him that has remained a permanent fixture on the driveway ever since.

The normal household dramas are unfolding. Standing at a safe distance, I observe Mum, a seasoned cook, by the stove with her sleeves rolled up and a determined expression on her face. Pots are simmering, and the ingredients all laid out. Hovering nearby is Grandad, a short and stocky man, his rounded belly a testament to his love for good food and excess drinking. Lined with age, his face carries a certain vibrancy. His deep-set eyes of a steely grey can shift from a piercing, serious gaze to a twinkling, mischievous glint in an instant. His bushy eyebrows often change with his moods, arching in surprise or knitting together in concentration or concern. He's the self-appointed sous-chef, with a penchant for meddling and offering unsolicited advice.

Peering into the bubbling pots, Grandad slips a finger in and tastes it. With a hint of playfulness, he announces, "A pinch more salt wouldn't hurt."

"Grandad, I've got it covered," Mum replies. Grandad's culinary contributions are more like interruptions, as he continually reaches for ingredients or rearranges utensils. His enthusiasm is undeniable, but it's testing, and I can see Mum's patience leaving the room fast. Trying to maintain her composure, Mum looks Grandad straight in the eyes and says, "I appreciate your help, but I really need some space here, now get out of my bloody kitchen!" Grandad replies with a sulky tone, "I was just trying to help, yew know." That's my cue to rescue the situation, so I shout out to him to join me in the living room.

Grandad's a complicated man - that's what I've concluded over the years. He has different sides to him that leave you confused. He has a fun, childlike manner mixed with a darker side that he hides well. He wants everyone to see the fun - loving person he so desperately presents himself as, but there are layers to this man.

Grandad reluctantly joins me in the living room, disappointed he wasn't needed in the kitchen. He looks at me, and like some all-knowing oracle, says, "I sense it I do, I feel it."

"What?" I ask.

"I just know," he responds, now with a cocky stance.

He drags me to one side as if this next part of the conversation is definitely not for Mum's ears. Blunt and to the point, he probes with a whispering tone, "You've been spotted staring, gazing in the direction of a young lady. People are starting to talk Tim, I'm surprised she's not rung the bloody police yet," he laughs uncontrollably. "What's all this about, lad?"

One thing about Grandad, he knows everything and everyone's business. He has a friend called Max, they're known as the old boys. There used to be three of them back in the day and they were inseparable. Clive was the third member of the old boy's crew but he moved away some years ago and I've never got to meet him. I don't think Grandads stayed in touch as he never mentions him, however I'm sure I've heard Max chatting with Clive on the phone now and again. Max owns the boatyard where I work. The pair of them have spent all their lives in the area. They're best friends and always have been. They gossip and hold regular meetings at The Salty Seagull pub and The Lace and Lime café. Mentally stuck at fourteen years old, they regularly disappear for days, sometimes weeks. It's wholesome, nostalgic, and beautiful, however Mum calls Grandad selfish, saying he has no sense of responsibility. Mum and Grandad have a strange relationship.

I realize Sam must be Grandad's source! Sam's also a gossip, although he'd never admit it.

"Grandad, she's amazing! She's beautiful, I can't help myself. It's a feeling I can't explain, I find myself just fixed in a trance-like stare whenever I see her."

I pause, take a deep breath, and exhale with a sense of overwhelming sadness.

"Ere what's wrong son?" Grandad asks, with a more soft and caring voice.

"I've not even spoken to her Grandad, and yet I feel so invested in her. It's as if I've known her all my life. I think about her all day every day. I can't focus or function Grandad, I'm a bloody mess." A little embarrassed, I continue, "I even go to places I think she'll be with the hope of seeing her. I've become a secret stalker! It's not good; perhaps I am a weirdo." I look at Grandad with pleading sincerity. "Grandad, am I a weirdo?"

He responds with a glint in his eye, "Yew've always bin a weirdo lad." I sink into the sofa, Grandad steadily follows. "She doesn't even know me, I could be invisible to her. She might even have a boyfriend. She might be married. What if she isn't even interested in boys? Oh, I don't know!" A repeat of that deep, sad breath leaves my chest again, and I just stare past him expressionless.

Grandad responds with an investigative tone, "Well lad, I've done the research and the groundwork for yew." Grandad seems chuffed with himself, he has that look upon his face. "She's not married and ain't got a boyfriend, tha' much I know. But I'll leave it down to yew to find out what bus she's on."

How can I be so excited yet so sad at the same time? What's wrong with me? A set of conflicting emotions constantly flip-flopping in my mind, my stomachs like a washing machine set on fast spin. Honestly, I'm not in a good place with this love stuff. The moment is interrupted by Mum shouting from the Kitchen. "Tea's on the table!"

Through the noise and conversations during tea time, all I can hear is the voice of Bob Marley singing 'Is This Love?' on repeat. I spend most of the time pushing my food from one side of my plate to the other, in a love-stricken daze.

After tea, Grandad ushers me to a safe space away from Mum's ears. "Son, therr's only one way you're truly gunna put this to the test. Yew'll 'ave to talk to her. Only then yew'll be able to decide if this is fate, real, the law of attraction, true love… or jus' a fantasy dream world which will confirm tha', yes you're truly a weirdo." Grandad then rests his hand on my shoulder with a gentle grip, a change of tone, softer, he flips back into all-knowing oracle mode. "Yew must trust the process son. Trust tha' the universe will deliver wha' the universe sees fit for yew. If this is meant to be, then it's meant to be. Trust the process and allow nature to take its course." I nod, tentatively taking in his wise words. "Imagine yerself with her, a place that allows yew to talk to her. Only then you're gunna know if she's who yew wan' her to be." As Grandad's playing the role of a spiritual guru, suddenly I'm reminded of this Friday's surf school gathering. Could this be my moment? I hear an echo of Sam's voice in my mind, louder than ever: "Grow some balls Tim." Then, suddenly, Grandad slips straight back to Grandad mode. He concludes his words of wisdom with, "Make sure yew smell proper nice though. Help yourself to me aftershave, tha'll do it. The ladies love it," He winks and walks off, chuckling.

    I wake up in the morning from a restless sleep and remnants of dreams flickering around my head. Between Spiritual Guru Grandad's straight-talking words of wisdom, the great Bob Marley's lyrics and Sam's little comments, my mind is buzzing.

Chapter 5

Sink or swim

As the golden sun begins its slow descent beyond the horizon, a warm amber glow is casted over our picturesque beach, known by the locals as Bottom Beach. A gathering of free-spirited souls come together for their love of the sea, good food, music, and friendships. The crackling bonfire stands as the centrepiece, sending sparks dancing into the evening sky. Its flickering flames cast playful shadows on the faces of those gathered, whilst sending an enchanting glow out to the sea and beyond. Stories, laughter and dreams are exchanged. Their voices carried by the gentle breeze. Calm waters stretch out like a vast liquid canvas. Some, sit on longboards, their feet dangling in the clear crystalline water, as if in quiet communication with the sea. I sit engulfed in the moment, my eyes scanning, but I haven't spotted Alice yet. Perhaps she isn't coming after all. I wander over to speak to Dylan, another lifelong friend of ours. Dylan's a unique character: a small-time weed connoisseur, the nicest person you'll ever meet with such a pure and beautiful heart.

Dylan's laid-back demeanour and infectious smile make him instantly likable, and able to make those around him feel at ease. His long blonde hair is usually pulled back in a messy bun, his eyes a vibrant green that sparkle with a carefree and adventurous spirit. He's a good-looking fella for sure, our Dylan is.

"Wasson dude?" he shouts as I walk towards him. He grabs me hold and wrestles a man hug. We sit, he passes me a spliff. I draw a smooth breath, inhale the sweet-smelling weed, and pass it back. Sam, from some distance, raises his head, catching a whiff and joins us. "Give us a puff man" he asks with a cheeky grin on his face. "Have you seen her yet Tim?" Not missing a trick, Dylan's on this comment. "Her, who's this her then?" They begin to chatter as if I weren't present, scripting my life's plans and journey, laughing and jesting about my secret love for Alice.

Suddenly, out of nowhere, a person flings them self excitedly over me. It's Daisy. It's as if she's seen a movie star or someone famous has turned up. She's so excited, beaming with a massive smile on her face. "She's here!" Jumping all over me rolling me into the sand, she shouts "SHE'S HERE!" Sam and Dylan immediately stand up like meerkats, sweeping the surroundings. "There, just out there" Daisy points, to a small group of people standing on the edge of the sea, holding longboards.

All three spring into action. Daisy brushing the sand off me, Sam turning into a hairstylist, flattening and shaping my hair. Looking directly at me full of emotion, Daisy says "My handsome boy, you go get her!"

"You've got this bro," Dylan reassures me as he forces the spliff into my mouth and says, "breathe." I take a long toke and feel the warmth of the smoke fill my chest. "Just be yourself mate."

I stumble forward glancing back over my shoulder to see the three of them looking straight at me with stern looks on their faces. Dylan's hands shooing me on. I look up to the sky and the night stars asking for... What? Help? Confidence? A miracle? Anything! I head towards the sea's edge, I start to feel myself relax, my anxiety levelling out to something resembling calm. Have my prayers been answered? Or is it just the weed kicking in? Taking one more deep breath for luck, I approach Alice and a few others from the surf school.

As I approach, Maddie spots me. "Hey Tim, what an amazing night!"

I reply, "Cornwall never disappoints," and join them, looking out to the ocean with wonder.

Alice says, "I feel so lucky to be part of this. It reminds me of home." This is my chance.

"Home?" I ask. "Where's home?"

"Australia," she replies.

"What brings you to Cornwall?"

"Dad's work."

Overwhelmed by her presence, I've completely forgotten to introduce myself.

"I've seen you around," Alice says. "You're a friend of Sam's, right.? You live here then?"

Now melting inside, awkwardly I respond, "Born here and never left." I nervously laugh a little. She smiles and I continue, "Sam's more like family, plus his hot chocolates are just the best!"

"Agreed!" Alice replies enthusiastically, breaking her glance out towards the sea and now looking directly at me with a natural sparkle in her eyes, "I'm Alice."

"It's nice to finally meet you properly, I'm Tim," I extend my hand out in an awkward attempt to shake hers. What a knob, who shakes hands anymore? Luckily, she shakes mine and chuckles. We hold each other's glance for what feels like forever. I'm sure she could hear my heart beating, for at that moment it's louder than the drumming back on the beach around the fire.

Alice leans down and gracefully slides her longboard into the calm clear water and looks back at me. "You coming?" I nervously walk out to my waist and climb onto the board that Alice is sitting on so naturally, like it's an extension of her very being. Beneath me, the soft, gentle waves lap around my legs, above, a mesmerising tapestry of stars. The moon, full, casts a silver pathway across the sea, illuminating Alice's face with a gentle glow. I look at her, "You know, I've always been fascinated by the night sky, there's something so..." I search for the right words, "grounding about it."

"I feel the same way; the vastness of the sky puts everything into perspective." The water gently rocks beneath us as we talk and talk, it's as if we've known each other forever. A complete comfort and ease. I'm trying hard not to stare at her longer than normal, but it's difficult. In the night-lit sky, she's even more beautiful. We share stories and laugh so naturally. I don't know why I was so nervous about talking to her. Grandad was right, I should have just trusted the process and believed in myself more.

I try to imitate her Australian accent, she splashes water over me in a playful manner. So, it begins! I repay her with a barrage of dark blue water. She leans forward pushing me in retaliation and I tumble backwards, losing my balance and sliding into the cold embrace of the ocean with a splash. One moment of joy replaced with blind panic and uncontrollable fear, playing out in slow motion as I sink down, the colours of the undercurrent flickering under the night sky adding to my overwhelming sense of dread. Instinctively I start to kick and fling my arms around wildly, driven by distress. My head rises above the water where I gasp for air, quickly dropping back under the layers of changing motion and light, I struggle to stay afloat. The world above is distorted as my imagination takes over my whole being. Is this how Dad felt in his last moments of life? Suddenly I feel a change of movement within the ocean, swirling bubbles surround me. Alice jumps in, grabs me hold and pulls me to the surface. "It's okay," she says, her voice calm and soothing above the sound of the lapping water caused by my chaos. "I've got you, just relax and I'll help you." Alice calmly floats me back to the longboard and helps me up. Embarrassed, while catching my breath and coughing up salty seawater, I say, "So, yeah, I can't actually swim."

Alice guides the longboard back to the shoreline and helps me to the water's edge. Still coughing up that now-familiar taste of salty water, I look at her standing tall with the moonlight bouncing off her silhouette.

Alice laughs and says, "That was hectic, you had me worried then! I thought you were messing around. It wasn't until I saw the fear on your face that I realised you were serious. Why did you come out with me knowing you can't swim? In fact, hold on, you live in Cornwall, you spend most of your time at the beach and you can't swim?" Alice's face looks confused and surprised.

Overwhelmed by the experience of nearly drowning and with flashbacks of the dark deep ocean, I have to find a logical response. "I just... never learned."

With a very calm voice, "No dramas. I'll help ya. Are you up for that Beach Boy? Do you wunna learn to swim?"

My tone now hesitant and childlike, "Yes please!" Alice playfully pushes herself into me, "You had me scared then for a bit Beach Boy." It seems I've a new nickname: 'Beach Boy.' I kinda like it.

We sit on the water's edge, exchanging our experiences of the night's events. "You're an interesting one." Looking intrigued and with a warmth in her eyes, she leans across and gives me a reassuring hug. Despite the chilly evening air, she's warm, and her embrace is firm but gentle. She smells of the ocean and something sweet, floral even. Whatever it is, it's intoxicating.

Alice stands up, "I have to go. It's been an

adventure Beach Boy! Get some rest, you'll need it for your swimming lessons." Laughing, she picks up her longboard and starts to walk back towards the car park.

I sink back into the sand. Lying there, I watch her fade into the distance, her outline slowly becoming a shadowy shape in the darkness. Inhaling, trying to keep her smell locked into my senses, I jump up from the sand suddenly full of life. The world's orchestra starts to play "Wonderwall" loud, as if it senses my emotions. I find myself alone, dancing round and round, singing loudly. What an evening! I nearly drowned in front of the most amazing and beautiful soul I've ever met. One way to make an impression, I guess!

Eventually, I make my way home. I open the front door, careful so as not to disturb anyone. As I walk into the sitting room, a little side lamp reveals Grandad's silhouette. He's fast asleep on the sofa. I often find him like this, curled up and fully dressed, surrounded with cushions like he's in a nest. I slowly and quietly walk through the sitting room towards the kitchen, trying not to disturb him. Before I can even make it half way across the room, he must've sensed my presence and sits bolt upright. "About bloody time lad! I've bin waiting for yew all night." He lowers his tone and volume, remembering it's late, and continues, "How's it gone son?" He moves some of the cushions and gently slaps the sofa, indicating for me to sit with him. I sit down alongside him, only for him then to say, "Actually, son, before yew sit down and tell I everything, put tha' kettle on and grab them biscuits."

We sit drinking tea as I tell him all about my evening's events. The beauty of Grandad is that he's such a great listener; how many people really listen to each other anymore? People seem so distracted and preoccupied, you can see it in their eyes. He has that ability to make you feel important, heard, and valued.

"I told you dint I lad, yew needed to learn to swim bloody years ago?"

Chapter 6
Drifting between dreams and reality

Whilst heading into work the next morning, I relive the night before over and over in my mind. I finally worked up the courage to speak to Alice and what did I do? Somehow, I managed to almost drown. A wave of embarrassment crashes over me followed by a small smirk as I'm reminded of Alice's kind and authentic nature. I wonder if she's thinking about me too. Caught in a daydream, I'm going through every moment, step by step, playing back the night's events as if it were a movie: skipping, rewinding, pausing, and fast forwarding all over the place. I can hear 'Wonderwall' playing as the backing track. How she looked at me, her smile, the contact, the hug... Oh, the hug! Her smell, which has unfortunately now become a memory. When will I get to smell her again?

To help ends meet I have two jobs that I juggle. I work at the boatyard cleaning the boats and getting the scuba diving equipment ready for tourists eager to see the delights of the Cornish coast. I also help in the pub kitchen and behind the bar at The Salty Seagull. Today however, it's boat cleaning duties.

Arriving at the boatyard, Sadie appears from behind stacks of weathered lobster traps and crab pots. "Morning!" she almost sings. Sadie is spritely on these early mornings. She's probably already been up for hours, Sadie loves a morning swim. I don't know what we would do without her to be honest, she's one of a kind. Max shouts out to her with his normal gravelly, weathered voice, "Sadie, wherr's tha' bloody tea, yew said yew were making?"

"On its way boss!" Max, the owner of the boat yard, is Grandad's best friend. "Tim, walk with me whilst I get his lordship's tea". As we walk through an entanglement of boats, Sadie asks. "Have you heard the news?"

"No, what news?"

"About the surf school. Jim, the owner, says he may have to close it due to the lack of customers this year. He came over and was talking to Max in the workshop. Who would have thought it?" She says. I wander off to find my job sheet for the day, but all I can think about is Alice. She can't leave, not now, I'm only just getting to know her.

The boatyard's charm extends to a weather-worn building known as the workshop cladded in old wood. Its planks, once a rich brown, now faded to a silvery grey. The office is situated just a few meters away from the workshop, it doesn't look like anything special on the outside but inside is Max's museum of things.'

Stumbling through the door, I find Max sat in one of the well-worn armchairs rolling a fag as he waits for his tea. He doesn't even lift his head as I come in, instead he mumbles "Fatla genes?"

"All good thanks boss." I reply, as I sit to join him with my job sheet in hand.

Inside the office is a large rustic table, a couple of well-worn arm chairs and odd bits of random furniture that Max has collected over the years. Every time I come in here, I notice more and more things he keeps adding. The office is also where Max keeps his rum supplies.

"Max, is it true that the surf school may have to close?"

"Can't see bloody how! They seem busy enough to me. I told tha' Jim, try running a boatyard mate if yew think yew've got it tough!" He huffed out an exasperated half-laugh. "yew know what these young'uns are like Tim, always fucking moaning about something." He gets up and walks off, whistling Trelawny.

Max is a robust man, nobody's really sure of his age but I reckon he's in his early seventies he has an aura of rugged resilience. His hair, a tangled mass of grey, is usually tucked under a tired cap that has seen better days. Not a sensitive, understanding kind of guy; he thinks everyone else has it better than him. He lives alone and has no one other than us and Grandad. He has a very dry sense of humour which can easily be misinterpreted. With a slight limp, it's clear he's lived a hard, colourful life. Deep lines carved in his sun-bronzed skin from years spent braving the elements, his nautical tattoos now faded. His eyes, a sharp, penetrating blue, that twinkle with mischief. Max is a pirate, really. There's no doubting it, it's in his blood.

*

Jobs done for the day, I head off to see Sam at the café.

He sees me approaching. "Good night last night then, bro?" he asks while playfully punching me. "Someone said earlier they heard you nearly bloody drowned, you dick! Bet your new Aussie bird was impressed with that then! What were you doing out in the sea anyway, you do know you can't bloody swim?" Laughing uncontrollably now, he flings his arm around me, pulls me in tight, and asks for all the details. I talk him through the adventures of last night, remembering Sam's probably Grandads informant so I refrain from telling him every single detail. I stop occasionally to allow him time to compose himself from laughing so much, he thought the whole thing was hilarious.

He asks "So, you seeing her again?"

I reluctantly answer, "Yes," feeling exposed and vulnerable, pausing to find the right words, "She's offered to teach me how to swim."

"That's bloody brilliant, bloody brilliant! Your second date's a swimming lesson. Best get yourself some armbands and a new pair of budgie smugglers; all the dudes wear them in Aus. I can't wait to tell Daisy about this, can't bloody wait." I try to say it's not a date, but by this time he's laughing so much he's tuned out. As Sam walks away, he shouts back, "You best not tell Dylan, you'll never live it down!".

I hear him mutter to himself, "Swimming lessons, bloody brilliant."

*

A couple of days go by and I haven't seen or heard from Alice. Should I be concerned? Perhaps she's had second thoughts about teaching me how to swim.

Working a late shift at The Salty Seagull is always a joy, especially if I'm working with Lydia. She's very upbeat and positive, an amazing person with a beautiful smile who cares deeply about the community. Her ambition is to one day, create a community space centred around mindfulness and well-being. I think that would truly suit her as a person but would certainly miss working with her. She's so inspiring and if I'm having a bad day, well she has the ability to lift anyone's spirits.

The low, timbered ceilings of The Salty Seagull give the impression of a ship's hold, nautical memorabilia adorn the walls: fishing nets, worn lifebuoys, and old faded photographs. The centrepiece of the pub is a robust wooden bar, its surface worn smooth by years of use. A chalkboard displays the day's catch, fresh seafood, and beer of the week. The aroma of local dishes fills the air. Grandad and Max are sitting in the corner looking shifty, leaning into each other and whispering as if they are sharing some kind of secret information or planning something.

"Gorthugher da," says Mr Martin as he walks in. "You busy?" He asks as he approaches me at the bar. Mr Martin comes from London but likes to pretend he's Cornish, at least he's trying to use our language even if it's just a few words.

It's never busy anymore. Busy in the height of summer; but for the rest of the year... well, quiet is an understatement. Still, I love working at The Salty Seagull. Every Tuesday the locals gather to sing sea shanties, their voices rising together in timeless harmony. With the deep hum of accordions, rhythmic strumming of guitars, and the haunting whistle of tin flutes weaving together a tapestry of sound. Tales of lost sailors and old fishing adventures drift through the pub, each song stirring nostalgia and pride in being Cornish.

As I go out back to change a barrel, I watch Mr Martin walk over to join Max and Grandad. Returning back into the front bar, the door opens and in walks Alice with some of the other surfing instructors. My heart races, and I feel giddy at seeing Alice again. What if she ghosts me? I try to compose myself. "Hi guys, what you having?" I ask. One of them sniggers to the other, I guess they heard about the drowning episode then. Alice looks stunning, she's wearing a pair of dungarees and Doc Martin boots, her hair thrown up in a messy bun. I lean forward, hoping to get a good sniff of her, I understand that seems weird but the memory of her smell has now fully faded and I need a new fix.

"G'day, Beach Boy," she says, smiling.

"Hi Alice, what can I get you?" As she places her order, I don't hear anything. I'm actually sniffing deeply, trying to recapture her smell. Sure enough, her intoxicating, scent fires through my nose and hits all of my senses, It's like an explosion. Don't judge me!

"Sorry, what's that?" I have to ask her to repeat it as I'm distracted by sniffing. She places her order and as I pour the drinks she asks "You still wanting a swimming instructor then?"

"Sure!" I reply, quietly grinning and slightly embarrassed.

"Cool, I'll pick you up tomorrow evening then. Say... eight?"

"Eight's good, our house is the one on the corner, you can't miss it, it's the one with the bloody big boat on the driveway."

"Bloody big boat, house on the corner, got it!" With a quirky little salute and a glint in her eye she takes her drinks and goes to sit down with her friends. I watch them as they chat, Alice and her friends seem worried about something. I'm guessing the news about the surf school could be true after all.

*

The next day, I tell Grandad about the surf school news, thinking if anyone knew, he would. Sure enough, he confirms that he'd spoken to Jim. The school wasn't doing so well. I use this as the perfect moment to tell him I'm due to see Alice tonight, his face lights up. "Right," he announces as if he's got a master plan already. "Do yew want some solid advice?"

"Sure," Grandad's going to give it to me anyway, right?

"First thing, don't trust tha' Dylan the pothead with any of this love stuff. Don't listen to any of his advice ee's a bloody strange one and can't be trusted. I taxed a joint off him last week, I'm sure ee stitched me right up. I lost best part of the day watching a seagull trying to eat a paper bag, not right really. Wherr yew going on this date then? What's ee idea?" Stumbling and slightly embarrassed, I search for an answer but, knowing I can't lie, I reveal the truth. "Well, she's going to help me learn to swim." Grandad's face looks surprised, but not wanting to embarrass me further, he replies, "Good, tha's good. Keep it simple, I like it. Plus, yew need to learn, how can yew be proper Cornish without being able to swim lad?" He pauses momentarily and then says, "So, wherr ee going then? Down Bottom Beach?"

"I didn't ask, she's picking me up at eight." Grandad looks puzzled. "This isn't a date, is it, Son?"

"No, Grandad. It's not a date."

"It's a swimming lesson, isn't it, Son?"

"Yes, Grandad, it's a swimming lesson."

"Ok, glad we've sorted tha' out," he replies.

"I'm still nervous though, you know how much I like her and I want to make a good impression, which I reckon will be hard while I'm flapping my arms about and taking on water."

"She must like yew Son. Otherwise, why bother offering to help yew?"

I consider this for a moment. "Anyway, honestly, I don't really care. I'm just looking forward to spending time with her, getting to know her better."

"Exactly Son, jus' time, get to know her. Suss her out a bit, check out wha' bus she's on and all tha'. Learn to swim, it'll be nice, get yew out the house."

Chapter 7

Swimming lessons

As eight o'clock draws close, I start to pace nervously - not just for spending time with Alice but because I've agreed to put myself in a very vulnerable position with learning to swim. I'm right out of my comfort zone. Running upstairs, I grab my jacket and spot a note and a bottle of aftershave Grandad has left me. The note simply says, "Good luck and wear this." I need the luck, but there's no chance I am wearing his aftershave! Not a chance. This isn't the nineteen seventies. As I make my way back downstairs, my mind races with doubt, Is this really a good idea? I do need to learn to swim, but from the most incredible girl I've ever met? Is this a bad idea? My thoughts are interrupted by a little beep from a car horn outside. I look out the window to spot a cool red Mini... Alice.

Driving through our beautiful Cornish countryside on our way to, well, wherever we're heading, I ask Alice about the surf school and what I'd recently heard. She confirms that Jim, the owner, had gathered all the staff and volunteers to announce that the school was struggling financially.

"How do you feel about it?" I ask.

"I'm hopeful something will turn up, I'm sure. You've always got to have hope in life."

We finally pull into a long driveway nestled deep in a valley, flanked by thick woodland and hedgerows. The canopy of trees overhead forms a natural tunnel, filtering the sunlight into a dappled mosaic on the ground. The driveway descends towards a campsite and holiday park, beautiful eyebrights greet us as we pull in. A sign, weathered by the Cornish elements, stands at the main entrance. Its once vibrant paint has faded to muted tones, a testament to countless seasons of sun, rain, and wind.

"Here we are," Alice says

"What a place," I reply.

"Friends of Mum and Dad own it, they've agreed we can use their pool for your swimming lessons. It closes at eight so it's just us." Walking into the swimming pool is like stepping back in time. With its high wooden beams and faded tiles, a sense of nostalgia comes over me. "This place looks like it hasn't changed since the eighties, I love it." I say mesmerised by the pools charm. Although the smell is something new to me, not the salty sea air I'm used to but a powerful chemical smell that isn't pleasant at all.

"I hope the water's warm and you have lots of patience, Alice."

"We'll give it a bloody good go," says Alice with a

gentle reassurance in her voice. She positions herself on the pool's edge, and dangles her feet into the water.

I walk cautiously to the changing room area and tried to focus myself. Breathe Tim, you've got this! Trying hard to block out any memories of my recent drowning experience, I head back to the pool. On returning, Alice is already in the water, swimming with an air of confidence. Her body moving smoothly and with minimal effort, every stroke and breath perfectly timed.

With rigid and hesitant movements, I position myself on the edge and dangle my legs in, adjusting to the temperature. The chemical smell is still overwhelming, hitting the back of my throat. Alice calmly swims towards me, hops out, and sits next to me, how incredible does she look in her swimming costume? I naturally find myself focusing on the drops of water gently rolling down her body. I need to get in the pool quickly before I embarrass myself if you know what I mean?

I look at Alice and say, "Thank you, this really means a lot, you giving up your time like this to help me."

Alice, with sincerity, says, "I want to help you Tim. The time we spent together the other night I really enjoyed it. It's as if I've known you forever. I'm comfortable with you, and that's very important to me, and yeah, you're kinda cute."

Cute, I'll take cute, but now I have to be brave. "Be gentle with me Alice." I slip into the water and feel reassured as my feet firmly plant themselves on the pools floor. Any physical desire I had when focusing on the drops of water rolling down Alice's soft skin vanish immediately.

"Step by step, no drowning on me tonight Beach Boy. I want you to bend your knees and rest your chin on the water but make sure to keep your feet on the floor. Get yourself used to the feeling of being surrounded by the water and learn to relax and breathe." She slips into the water next to me and reassuringly holds my hand. How could I concentrate? She's flipping holding my hand. The touch of her hand wrapping around mine makes me feel at ease and safe. I feel constricted and slightly disoriented as the water's force pushes back and forth against my body, a strange sensation I hadn't experienced before - well, other than the drowning thing, obviously.

"Well done Tim! Now, it's so important to stay relaxed, you're safe. You need to trust me, OK? I've got you."

"I trust you Alice."

"Now, I need you to hold onto the side of the pool and slowly push yourself out whilst lifting your legs from the bottom and kick them. Extend your arms and keep kicking. Keep your chin up at all times Tim, OK?"

I follow Alice's instructions, water laps against my face, but I, find myself somewhat floating. *Result!*

"Now Tim, when you're ready take a gasp of air and fill your lungs. Slowly lower your face into the water, but don't breathe when you're under, that won't be a good idea," she laughs. "Hold your head under for a few seconds, and without panic, raise your head back up and relax." Alice slid her hand under my body, acting as extra support whilst I'm franticly kicking and trying to stay afloat. The sensation is weird, and the sound was different than I expected - a diffused echo, muffled as my head went under the water. Alice removes her hand and somehow, I manage to stay afloat.

"Well done you, step one ticked. Now catch your breath and relax again. We need to do the same, but this time, when you're ready, let go of the side and gently push back. "You good?" Alice asks.

"Got it," I reply. I follow her instructions, and strangely, the whole process starts to feel more familiar. An hour or so soon passes, and my first proper swimming lesson hasn't been anywhere near as scary as I had thought. Alice is so calm and reassuring, I'm actually, enjoying it. Trying new things and getting out of your comfort zone is highly recommended apparently.

"We need to keep this up now Tim, every week, so you don't lose the gains you make."

*

Alice and I head back, all the way home we're just chatting and laughing. I love her accent, it captures me. We have so much in common, sharing the same values and beliefs. She's quite spiritual and sees the world in a similar way. Her positive outlook and attitude is refreshing and addictive. Arriving back at my house,

I lean over and give her a kiss on the cheek, "Thanks, Alice. I've had the best first swimming lesson. You're an amazing instructor."

She pushes me in jest, "No dramas Beach Boy. See you next week."

"Alice, where's the Beach Boy name come from?"

"Every time I see you, you're at the beach staring, I think mostly in my direction. So, I've nick-named you Beach Boy," she laughs.

That night, I sit in the garden and look up into the sky. A clear Cornish sky is so beautiful; an inky, star-studded canopy, the air crisp and carrying the faint scent of salt from the sea, replacing the chemical smell of the pool. I feel a sense of achievement. I was able to overcome my fear of being in the water, even feeling a sense of calmness and enjoyment. I'm a little bit proud of myself, if I'm honest. My mind wanders towards Alice, how her eyes lit up when she talked about her passions. Our conversation flowed effortlessly and she listened intently. She's naturally strong and reassuring, and she possesses a unique blend of intelligence, humour, and kindness. Her spiritual awareness encourages me to look deeper into my own spiritual values and understanding. Ever since I lost Dad, and being exposed to such deep emotional trauma, I've felt connected to something, hard to describe. I value the simplest of things and have overwhelming moments of both joy and sadness. My emotions can spiral in a heartbeat. I can see beauty in everything. I can also, however, see the pain and sorrow in the world. I think I just value life so much, and I sense Alice has the same connections. The way she talks about things as if she feels them, resonates with me.

A shooting star passes overhead. Its brightness offering a feeling of hope, excitement, and the sweet anticipation of what might become of Alice and me.

*

Throughout the following week, I hear more and more about local businesses struggling. It seems like everyone's talking about their hardships, trying to make ends meet. A common theme of financial struggle is emerging within our community, which is really worrying for everyone. In Cornwall so many houses are second homes, there are luxurious and expensive hotels, restaurants, art galleries, and yes, you can buy a posh coffee for ten pounds if you wish. This all contributes to the economy, which is of course welcome, but so much of Cornwall doesn't have that kind of wealth. Seasonal jobs, low pay, unemployment, and limited affordable housing is our hidden reality.

But I guess it depends on what you consider to be wealth and richness. As a local I believe Cornwall has it in abundance and by this, I mean; clean air, beautiful natural landscapes, the ocean, the sky, the light, the people, and its proud history. It's not until you've been kissed by the Cornish air that you become captured by her magic and can't leave - she won't let you.

*

A message comes through on my phone.

Alice: *Beach Boy, just checking if you're still on for tomorrow night? xx.*

Tim: *Of course, can't quit now, I've been practising in the bath xx.*

Alice: *Pick you up at eight then xx.*

My second lesson goes really well! I can stay afloat, and I've moved a few feet on my own. Progress is slow but steady, and my confidence is growing. I feel more comfortable in the water, I'm getting used to the motion and the way the water hugs you. The smell, however, I don't think I'll ever get used to that. The time spent with Alice just keeps confirming what an amazing person she is. She's such a genuine character, we seem to be able to open up equally and share our time together in such a natural way.

On the way home, I wrestle with the idea of inviting her in. I don't want our time together to end, but I also don't want to be pushy. I pluck up the courage. "Alice, do you want to come in for a coffee or tea? In fact, I've got some hot chocolate if you prefer."

"I'd love to."

Chapter 8
Opening up

Alice comments on the boat in the front garden, "That's Grandad's, he can't seem to let it go for some reason." We sit in the kitchen talking whilst drinking hot chocolate. She asks about my family, a conversation I knew would come up eventually.

"Well, it's my Mum, Grandad and me. Sadly I lost my Dad when I was only nine years old."

"I'm sorry to hear that Tim," Alice responds calmly, reaching out to hold my hand. I look directly into her eyes and see the honest soul that I've become so fond of. "It's OK, it was a long time ago. He was my hero and was always there for me, we had such fun and adventures." Alice then asks, "How did he die Tim?"

"It was a diving accident." My gaze drifts, as if searching through a distant past that seems both vivid, hazy and somewhat lost in time.

"It must have been really tough for you?"

"For years, I've felt this immense void, like a piece

of my heart had been taken away. I miss him so much. At first, I was angry, frustrated, and hated everyone. I felt it was my fault and that I needed to be punished. I was destructive. If it wasn't for Mum, Grandad, my friends, and Mrs Appleton, who knows where I would have ended up?"

"Mrs Appleton?" Alice asks.

"She was my therapist through that difficult time, she gave me some advice in one of our sessions, while we ate biscuits, that really helped me"

"What was the advice she gave you that made such a difference?" Alice asks.

"She asked me this – 'if you found an animal or something that was so special, a one off, unique, a true miracle, would you treat it right, with kindness, and never hurt it?' She explained that I am that special, unique thing. There is not another me in the whole wide world. And I needed to realise how special and beautiful I am. She told me that I needed to start looking after myself with that same amount of care and dedication."

I look at Alice and notice a tear rolling down her cheek. I continue. "That was the breakthrough moment Alice, from that point on, I understood the value of life and how I was responsible for my own actions. I was responsible for looking after myself."

Alice wipes the tear from her cheek and slowly leans towards me, her eyes half closed. As our lips press together the contact is soft and intimate. The warmth and moisture of our lips creates a surge of passion as our kiss extends. Alice's fingers trace gently over my face whilst our breath quickens, each touch a blend of tenderness, urgency now pulsing between us as our bodies push tightly together. The kiss lingers and our hands wonder. As our lips slowly part, I'm left feeling light headed. This is a moment I'd dreamt of and it didn't disappoint. She's an amazing kisser!

"You're special Tim, I saw that the very first time we met, I could feel it, it's in your eyes, and in your voice."

"Thank goodness for that, you've moved into my mind and taken up residence, and I kind of like it."

As the conversation continued Alice explains why she and her family left Australia and moved to Cornwall. "Dad's a marine researcher working on a new project. I was sad to leave home I had the option to stay, but I chose to be with my family and was excited for a new adventure."

"How does Cornwall compare to Australia?"

"Australia's huge compared to England and quite diverse from area to area. We lived in the Kimberley region, in the North-West. I grew up near a place called Broome. My Dad's Indigenous, Aboriginal, a member of the First People. He taught me how to love the land, to stop and connect with nature, and we spent all our time in the bush or by the sea. The beaches are beautiful; you would love them. There's a beach not far away known as Eighty-Mile Beach but it's actually 220 kilometres. In November and December, sea turtles arrive to lay their eggs, it's amazing to see. It's tropical, hot, often in the thirties, but when it rains, it rains. The sea's much warmer than Cornwall, I would love to take you one day. What took some getting used to, is how small and close everything is here, I felt so claustrophobic. Broome is a bit more remote, and you can easily escape people. The earth is a beautiful red colour. Our area is also well-known for its amazing pearls, I've always loved pearls."

"It sounds amazing, I would love to go! I've never been abroad, actually, I've never been on a plane." I add with a slightly embarrassed expression.

"That's one thing you'll have to put on your bucket list then Tim."

"Has there been any news regarding the surf school?" I ask.

"No, not really, but I hope it doesn't close. I love it, it's such an amazing thing to see people enjoying the water. Surfing's an exhilarating dance with the sea." Alice beams, as she explains the essence of surfing, almost reliving the moment.

"When you catch your first wave, it's an adrenaline rush - the feeling, the surge of the ocean's power beneath you, when your board becomes an extension of your body, time loses relevance. I can't wait to teach you," Alice says, with an excited look upon her face.

"Hang on there, I've not completed my first length yet!" I laugh, trying to imagine the sense of achievement when I do.

"You're doing really well Tim," Alice assures me. "My

mission is to get you confident enough to get you in the sea and who knows, one day catch your first wave surfing."

I try to envisage myself standing up tall on a board catching a wave, looking cool. Then I crash back to reality, lowering my expectations back to completing my first length of the swimming pool.

"Would you be up for getting together sometime during the week?" I ask. "I'd love to take you to a very special place."

"Sure," Alice says, "I've got to head off now but I'll message you, and we can arrange a time to visit this special place of yours. Thanks for the hot chocolate Beach Boy."

*

The next day, I receive a message: and I look at the time, it's 4:44. Don't you just love it when numbers appear in sequence? Angel numbers, some say.

Alice: *G'day, happy Tuesday Beach Boy. I'm free all-day Wednesday if you are? xx.*

Tim: *Happy Tuesday! I'm looking forward to taking you to my special place. Fancy meeting at Sam's Café, 12ish? It's a bit of a walk but worth it xx.*

Alice: *12 it is. xx.*

I prepare a small picnic and head to Sam's. I feel a little nervous as I want to take Alice to the bench where my Dad and I last sat together before his accident. I've never taken anyone there before, I've kind of kept it to myself.

*

The sky's clear and the wind calm, it's a beautiful Cornish day. Arriving at Sam's, he looks distressed. "You okay man?"

"Yo, dude. Yeah, fine thanks mate. Just frustrated, so bloody frustrated! Our overheads are spiralling, because people aren't spending their hard-earned cash like they used to. This was a thriving little business." He stands up aggressively and randomly shouts. "We need your cash!" He sits back down, as if this was normal behaviour. I feel his frustration; he's normally an upbeat, optimistic character. It's such a shame to see Sam this way, but a sign of the times I guess.

"It'll be alright Tim, we'll find a way. Hot chocolate mate?" he grins, knowing the answer and scurries off, talking to himself, "It'll be alright, it's always alright."

I see Alice walking towards Sam's Café. "Hey you," she says as she gets a little closer. She leans in for a kiss, which now feels so natural, the best feeling ever. She sits down next to me, and as Sam peers out, he shouts, "Hot chocolate Alice?"

"Sure, why not! Thanks Sam"

We take our hot chocolates and walk along the beach. It feels right to reach down and hold her hand,

I look at her for reassurance, permission if you like, which is granted as she smiles back at me. As we walk, we talk about the community and how we've noticed that the majority of people seem a little low at the moment. Life just seems so much tougher for people nowadays. I tell her about Sam randomly shouting out. If only there was a way to help him and other people in our community.

"Where you taking me Tim? Where's this special place?"

"You'll see, not far now."

We stroll along the edge of the world, where land and water meet in an enchanting embrace. The vast expanse of the ocean stretches out to the distant horizon, flickering and dancing light bounces off the different shades of the dark blue water. I'm so grateful to be spending time with someone who sees the same beauty in life as I do.

A thirty-minute walk brings us up and over to the coastal path. The views are stunning, the countryside around us is a tapestry of colour, dotted with patches of vibrant wildflowers: purple heather, and clusters of delicate white daisies. Butterflies flutter between the blooms, their wings flashing in the sunlight. The cliffside drops steeply into the turquoise water, wave's crashing against the rocks below with power. There in the distance is my favourite place, my heart naturally feels warmth whenever I approach.

"This was the last place I shared with my Dad all those years ago".

"Where?"

"Just there." I point to a bench perched just a few steps away from the coastal path. The wood, aged by the relentless embrace of the sun and the sea's salt, bears the scars of countless seasons, its surface smoothed by the elements' tender yet powerful touch. She grips my hand a little tighter, sensing my emotion as we walk closer and take a seat. The bench's backrest and wooden slats offer comfort and familiarity to me whilst looking out to the world.

I have spent so many hours gazing out to sea and beyond, searching for reassurance and confirmation about my life's journey. Alice sits as if she also senses the bench's importance. She gazes out to the horizon where the sea and sky meet in a seamless, ethereal union, blurring lines.

"It's beautiful, thanks for bringing me to your special place Tim."

"I sat here looking out to sea and had my last moment with Dad, it seems like a lifetime ago but also as if it was just yesterday." We both take a moment to look out into the beauty, a moment of reflection and silence shared together.

"I remember the conversation we had as clear as day, Dad wanted to tell me a story. He seemed so determined for me to know. The story he told seemed to have a meaning, a reason for sharing," I point out to the vast ocean and say. "Out there, Alice, my Dad told me about a Spanish ship called 'The Hope.' He said that The Hope sank in an almighty storm, but this was no ordinary ship. It was laden with treasure, gold, silver, and precious gemstones. Dad then said very clearly and with intent that the ship was waiting to be discovered by anyone brave enough to seek it." I look at Alice, pausing, waiting for a response.

"Do you think it was just a story, or do you think your Dad knew something?"

"I think he knew something."

"Have you spoken to anyone else about this Tim?"

"No, a few years ago I tried to talk to Grandad but he quickly shut me down which left me suspicious. I've got a feeling Grandad's hiding something, he had an angry look on his face, not something Grandad wants you to see - he usually keeps his anger hidden well."

"If your Dad was right and there is a Spanish ship with treasure out there, then who else knows, and is it still there waiting to be discovered?"

"I don't know Alice, but I feel that Dad wanted me to know for a reason, and I owe it to him to find out."

I presented my picnic. Sandwiches, salad and fruit pots. Alice and I sit talking and wondering if there truly is treasure out there waiting to be discovered.

"Dad told me that when the moon was bright and the sea calm, you could see the shape of the ship on the bottom of the sea and the treasure glinting."

"Imagine if we found treasure out there," Alice says. We stay and watch the sunset together lost in our imagination and intrigue.

Chapter 9

The truth

My swimming lessons are going well, and my confidence has truly grown. It's been several months now, and Alice seems keen to get me into the sea. It's my next step, I'm eager to finally feel the excitement of swimming in the open ocean rather than the confines of the swimming pool.

Alice assures me that I'm ready, and yes, I feel ready. Putting on a wetsuit for the first time is an experience. As I pull the suit over my limbs, the initial chill of the cold fabric hugging against my skin is strange, to say the least. Alice and I enter the calm water together, which gives me a sense of reassurance. After all, she's saved me once already. The buoyancy of the water lapping around me releases something inside of me, my inner child excited and ready for an adventure.

"Now Tim, be prepared. Although it's calm, the sea will have an undercurrent. The aim is to get you used to this sensation and to not go out of your depth. Keep your chin up to start with, and only put your head under the water when you feel ready. I'll swim along with you, it's important not to go too far because it's shallow for a while, but it drops off quickly in line with those rocks." Alice points to a rock formation.

It's truly amazing, and I feel more relaxed than I thought I would. The sense of freedom and the movement of the water is magical. We spend a while just swimming around and getting comfortable. Looking back to the shore's edge is a new sight for me and gives the sea and land a new perspective.

"Thanks Alice. This has been an amazing experience you've made possible for me."

"It's a whole new world for us to explore together," Alice responds. "Just wait, we'll have you using the snorkel next week and going out a bit further."

We walk back to Sam's Café to get changed. Sam pulls me to one side and asks how things between Alice and I are. I look over to Alice, sitting and talking to Daisy; I can only guess they're having a similar conversation. Daisy and Sam are almost the same person now; after years of being together, they've morphed into one. They both like knowing what's going on and all the latest gossip.

"It's going really well. We share so many of the same interests in life, and Alice is super adventurous, which is bringing me out of myself. She's always up for doing things and doesn't see the fear. I really like her Sam, and I think she likes me too."

Sam looks over towards the girls, "Well, we love her. If I had to match you with someone, it would be

Alice. She seems to have your best interests at heart and comes across as natural and super caring mate." Such a nice thing for Sam to say. I glance over to see Alice and Daisy laughing and getting along, which is a bonus since these people are like family to me.

*

That night, when I got home, I find the confidence to bring up the question regarding the Spanish ship with Grandad again. Last time did not go well, so I'm extremely nervous but determined to approach the subject once more.

"Grandad, I need to ask you something; it's been on my mind for a while now."

"Go on son, wha' is it?" Grandad's sitting at the kitchen table, carving a small piece of wood. Mum wouldn't be happy, Grandad always somehow leaves a mess, as if he doesn't see the small fragments of wood shavings left behind. I often tidy up after him before Mum gets home to avoid any arguments. The smell of wood shavings is familiar and helps put me at ease.

"It's about the story Dad told me the last time we spoke before his accident, the story of the sunken Spanish ship." Grandad doesn't take his focus off his carving and says nothing, as if he's preparing himself.

His carving knife slips off the wood and cuts deep into his hand. As if in slow motion, blood trickles down over his old, wrinkled knuckles. He looks up with a solemn stare, his piercing steely grey eyes seem darker, and a look of anger is on his face once again.

"Fetch I a cloth," he demands with a deep and pained tone. I pass him a cloth and he wrap's it around his cut tightly. Whilst staring at me, he says "Tis not to be talked about. Yew 'ave to leave it lad." He gets up and walks out so I follow him into the sitting room. He slumps onto the sofa, still clutching his cut hand with traces of blood now seeping through the cloth.

"Grandad, why do I need to leave it? Why's this such a difficult thing for you to talk about? This is important to me. It was the last thing Dad and I talked about. It was the last conversation we had together. He wanted me to know about the ship, Grandad. It was extremely important to him, and now it's important to me."

Grandad sits in silence. The atmosphere changes and a tear slowly roll's down his face, his eyes now reddened with sorrow.

He takes a deep breath and slowly exhales.

"Son, tis my fault, tis all my fault." He begins, with a crackle in his voice.

"What's your fault, Grandad? What is?"

"Me, it came from me."

"What did, Grandad?" It seems that he is talking in some kind of riddle that I can't make sense of.

He sinks even further into the sofa and, with a big sigh, repeats, "'tis all my fault." More tears roll down his cheeks as he inhales as if it was his last breath. There's a deadly silence, and I feel apprehensive, as if I'm about to be told something that is going to change everything.

He slowly looks up, with the saddest of eyes, "'ee's dead because of me." I slowly sit down in anticipation, I need to prepare for what's coming next. The light is naturally dimming as the day closes and the night begins. Every single moment is slow and enhanced; I can feel my heart beating within my chest. I'm scared, so scared. I remain quiet to allow Grandad time to compose himself.

"Ee wouldn't 'ave died if I hadn't told him about that bloody map and the shipwreck," Grandad says with the most haunting voice that echoes around my mind. Grandad, tired and remorseful, continues. His voice now slow and steady. "Many years ago, when clearing out my Dad's house after he passed away, I found a dark-stained wooden box with delicate Spanish words carved into it. I opened the box, and therr was a note and a map. On the top of the box, it said 'La Esperanza' which translated means 'The Hope.' Written on the note was an account of a man named Tristan Richards, dated 1789. The note described how a Spanish ship had sunk in a terrible storm, and Tristan and a man called William Thomas had discovered the remains," Grandad sighed deeply. "Twas a trade ship tha' also 'ad precious cargo. The note mentions the ship 'ad treasure, jewels, and gold. It said 'ow they came across the wreck and found the box. Inside the box was treasure but it slipped into the deep, dark water and was lost."

I sit listening intently, my mouth becomes dry and my hands sweaty. Despite the tension, there was a sense of intrigue and satisfaction that at last, I'm finding out the truth.

"How did your Dad come into possession of the box Grandad? And what about the map?" I ask.

Grandad takes a moment to prepare for the next part of his story, his eyes still wet and his posture weak and frail.

"Tristan, ee's a Richards, just like us son. Ee's our distant relative and that's 'ow the box has remained in the family all these years."

I stare into space, trying to process all the information. "This is a lot, Grandad—a lot to take in." I rise from my seat and start to pace, feeling both intrigued but overwhelmed.

Grandad determined to finish his story, a release for him after all these years of bottling it up, looks me straight in the eye with a solid stare and says, "I was the one who told yer Dad, showed him the map. I was the one who organised the dive. I was the one who took yer Dad to the wreck. If it weren't for me, ee'd still be alive today." An uncontrollable yelp of pain pours out as he slowly buries his head in his hands and his body deflates.

Shocked by this confession, I try to put all this information in some order. "How did he die, Grandad? How did he die?" I ask.

Grandad raises his head in remorse, "He never came

up Tim. They found him the next day washed up on the rocks."

I walk over and sit next to Grandad, putting my arm around him. He's cold and shaking. "Did he dive down Grandad? Is that how he died? Looking for the lost treasure?" Grandad just manages a nod to confirm. "I told the police before they started the search tha' we were out fishing and ee was practising diving. The coast guard found him dead on a rocky outcrop, washed up by the tide."

"Grandad, this can't be your fault. Dad knew what he was doing, and this was just an accident, just an accident Grandad." I'm shaking as I speak. Tears now rolling down my face.

"I never mentioned the treasure and the wreck Tim. I never told the police, not even your mum."

"Oh, Grandad, this has been so much for you to bear. Bless you." I squeeze him tight, feeling the burden he'd been carrying all this time.

I sit, feeling emotions of both anger and sadness; angry that I never knew this story, sad that this was a tragic accident and how Grandad had been carrying this guilt ever since. Speechless and dazed, I just sit rubbing Grandad's back calmly.

"I'm sorry son. I'm so, so sorry."

Silence and a thick dense atmosphere hangs in the room while we both sit there. We don't say or do anything, stuck in the moment of time with just our own thoughts. The night ends with Grandad falling asleep, exhausted. I pull the blanket over him, lean in and kiss his head, "Goodnight Grandad." I plonk back into the chair and just stare at him. All this time he's had to keep such a painful secret to himself, how did he do it?

Chapter 10

The box, the map and the boat

The next morning Grandad's nowhere to be found. "Where's Grandad?" I shout out to Mum.

"He's out, sitting on that bloody boat Tim. Go and talk to him; he doesn't seem himself." She hollers back.

I hurry outside. "The boat, Grandad? Is this the boat you used? Is this why you can't let it go?"

He just looks at me, but 'yes' is written all over his face.

We both sit in the boat, looking at each other, almost too frightened to talk. I look at him, "I love you Grandad." I reach out and give him a big hug. He had spent all this time carrying this burden and guilt, how had he managed?

"I was so scared that yew would blame me son. Yer Dad 'ad a strong mind, and when ee made it up, therr was nothing anyone could do. Yew remind me so much of him. Your Dad was adventurous and inquisitive, and after telling him the story and showing him the map, ee was determined and persuasive. Together, we thought we could find the treasure."

"Was anyone else involved Grandad?" I ask.

"The boat was your Dad's but we'd got the diving equipment from Max. Ee knew we were exploring wrecks but didn't know about the treasure. Yer Dad and I agreed not to tell anybody. That's why, after we lost yer Dad, I couldn't tell anyone; yew, your mum, anyone. We'd agreed no one should ever know, so I kept it all to meself."

"Did you find anything? Was there any sign of the wreck and the treasure?"

"Yer Dad went down several times. Ee said therr was a wreck, but it wasn't the Spanish ship. It made no sense. The map indicated tha' the wreckage was therr, but on the third dive down, your Dad never came back up. I sat for ages waiting, jus' waiting. Minutes bled into hours. I tried to leave several times but I had a feeling tha' if I left I wouldn't see him again so I jus' waited. The inquest determined that ee might have developed hypothermia and became disoriented, it said in the autopsy therr was a strong case suggesting ee may have passed out. I guess we'll never know son."

Sadness came over me and my heart feels heavy as I imagine Dad's last moments, alone, lost and confused. Separated from the world.

"Have you still got the map Grandad?"

"It's 'ere," he opens one of the storage boxes within the boat and pulls out the original Spanish box. It's beautiful to look at. The map's wrapped in cling film to preserve it, although it's certainly seen better days. I carefully unfold it. The paper yields with the delicate crackle of time-worn parchment. Its texture, once smooth, has evolved into a fragile and brittle surface, like the whisper of secrets held in your hands. The scent that arises is musty. a blend of history, reminiscent of old damp books. The carefully inked lines and markings, now faded with age, traced the details of the Spanish shipwreck. As I study it Grandad looks away, too emotional to engage. I pull out my phone and take several pictures.

"You're not to do this Tim," Grandad says with a strong, firm tone. "I've lost one person because of this fucking map and I'm not about to lose another." He picks up the map, folds it carelessly, puts it back within the protection of the cling film, and returns it to the box as if he is disgusted with it. The box captivates me with its beauty, the carvings and design are like nothing I've seen before. My heart picks up the pace as I feel a sense of both excitement and entrapment. I say nothing in response to his comment and just sit in silence. Deep down inside, he must know I'm not going to let this drop, and I also know that he won't either. We were kin and had the same determination, the same as Dad. I just need to think this through and work out a way to win him over. This is now too important to just let it be.

*

After my shift at the boatyard, I walk up to our bench and sit, looking out to sea. I wonder about the wreck and how Grandad and Dad used the map to find its location, but Dad said it wasn't there. I pull my phone out and look at the pictures I took of the map. Was this map even true? Was there really a ship with treasure out there or just a made-up story? The map shows the location, but something seems odd. The cliff edge marked on the map seems different. The map shows the shoreline and a beach area, the location was marked as the wreck being on the right of the bay. I study the it closer. I start to look at the cliff face and the natural shape of that area. This map is over two hundred years old, faded and certainly not easy to read. Something didn't seem right. The shoreline looks different, maybe some natural erosion and the retreat of the landscape over time has influenced the way I'm looking at it all. I reckon the ship could be out further. If the map was true we're in the right area but finding that ship was not going to be easy.

*

Arriving home that evening, Grandad's sitting in his usual spot at the dinner table and Mum's trying to prepare dinner while blocking out Grandad's interference. As I walk in, Mum announces, "Have you heard son? We're going to be famous."

"Famous?" I ask. "What's Grandad done now?" I laugh.

"Not Grandad you fool, the wreck." I watch

Grandad's eyes widen as he looks straight at me with a startled look upon his face, his bushy eyebrows drop with concern.

"What wreck?" I ask.

"It was on the radio on my way back from work. Apparently, a salvage company believes there's an old wreck off our coast, can you believe it? Later this year, they're planning to start exploring all around this area. Just imagine if they find anything. How exciting! We'll all be famous, it's about time we were put on the map for something." She says smiling.

As soon as dinner's finished, Grandad ushers me out to the front garden and into the boat. This now seems to be our secret discussion place.

"What's tha' all about?" he asks, still holding that scared look on his face.

"It can't happen Grandad, it just can't happen. That treasure's ours. It's in the family. It was always meant to be found by our family. Dad lost his life searching for that treasure, and I'm damned if I'm gunna sit by and watch some random salvage company take what's ours."

"Tha's what I was afraid yew were gunna say son," Grandad replies.

"You must feel the same way, you more so. You've been carrying this whole ship thing around with you for years."

Grandad, searching for the right words, replies

"You're right son." Suddenly, sitting bolt upright he declares "Tha's our bloody treasure, and your Dad did not lose 'is life for some other bugger to get therr hands on it. Right son, wha's the plan?" Excited by his response I continue, "We don't have long, and we need to do this right this time. It's me and you Grandad, not to be disrespectful, but we can't and shouldn't do this on our own. We need to bring others in to help, but who can we trust?"

"You're right, you've only jus' learned to swim," says Grandad with a sneaky grin. "And I can't go down, not with my bloody hips. We'll need a boat and scuba diving equipment as well," he adds.

"We have a boat right here."

"Not this boat," He replies, "This boat stays ere. Too many memories for this old girl to go back out therr again."

"Can we trust Max?" I ask.

Grandad laughs, "Max, tha' old pirate, ee's one of my dearest friends. Ee's a right grumpy old bugger."

"But can we trust him though?" I ask again.

"We can trust him. One thing ee's true to is his word and ee's got all the equipment tha' we need," Grandad winks.

"So that's me and the old boys. That's *great* that is, what a crew we have."

"Don't take the piss son," Grandad looks sternly in

my direction. "So, who yew bringing forward to join our motley crew then?"

"That's easy, Sam and Daisy. They're both strong swimmers, great divers and have no fear. They're adventure junkies in every way."

"Wha' about tha' Alice?" asks Grandad.

"Alice has to be part of it, she has all the experience. We also need Dylan, he's the brains. He's a great natural problem solver and a quick thinker." Grandads face displays a concerned frown "Dylan, not tha' fanny?"

"Not sure you can use the word fanny to describe people any more Grandad."

"Ee's definitely a fanny son," laughs Grandad. "Did I tell yew ee stitched me right up with tha' joint?"

"Yeah, you spent most of the day watching a gull eating a paper bag apparently. You shouldn't be smoking joints at your age Grandad, plus it *is* illegal." Grandad just shakes his head. "Can we trust 'em all son?"

"One hundred percent."

"Well, let's start with the obvious. We need to recruit our crew and keep our bloody fingers crossed they agree to this madness. I'll talk to the pirate," says Grandad, "and yew get them youngsters ready."

I message Alice straight away, asking her to meet me at the bench tomorrow afternoon. I get an instant reply with a smiley face and three kisses. Life's suddenly become much sweeter than yesterday. I've gone from two kisses to three. That extra one makes all the difference.

*

I arrive early at the bench, and study the map. The more I study it, the more convinced I am that our ship's out a little further than Grandad thinks. I look up and see Alice walking towards the bench, her face smiling. "So then Beach Boy, what's the importance of this meeting? I'm guessing it's not another picnic."

"You're going to have to take a deep breath for this one Alice, and keep an open mind." I show her the pictures of the map I'd taken. She looks closely, her gaze sharpens as she studies it, before looking out to the horizon.

"Is this what I think it is?" she asks, her voice a mix of disbelief and intrigue. "A map showing the ship your Dad told you about?"

"It is Alice."

"Where the hell did this come from?"

"It's been in the family for quite some time apparently." I feel a sense of pride mixed with trepidation as I delve into the story. "When Grandad's dad passed away, he found an old box at his house. Inside was this map and a note."

Alice's eyes widen as she processes the weight of the revelation. "Do you think your Grandad showed the map to your Dad Tim, and that's where he got the story about the Spanish shipwreck and treasure from? It came from your Grandad?"

"Yes, it was Grandad who told Dad and together they decided to go looking for it." I feel the past echoing in my chest, a mix of nostalgia and sorrow.

"Looking for it?" Alice's voice trembles with realisation. "Is that how your Dad died?"

"He died diving for the treasure," I respond. Alice pauses, her expression shifting as emotions wash over her. "Grandad finally opened up Alice, and told me everything."

Her eyes meet mine, softening with sympathy. "I'm so sorry," she whispers, reaching out to pull me into a hug. "How do you feel now, knowing how your Dad really died?"

"It's been very emotional" I admit, the weight of her question pressing down. "I knew he died in a diving accident out at sea, but obviously, I had no idea of the circumstances. Grandad never told anyone about the treasure, and still to this day, he's kept it a secret until now. Honestly I'm not sure how I feel - other than relieved to finally know the truth."

"Your Grandad has kept this a secret all this time?" Alice's eyes are wide, reflecting disbelief.

"Yes, not even Mum knows they were looking for treasure. It was just a diving accident - that was the final outcome, that's what everybody thinks."

"But they didn't find it?" she asks, her voice a whisper.

"No, they didn't. But it all makes sense to me now."

"But how did they know there was treasure in the first place?" she probes, the intrigue in her eyes burning brighter.

"The note Grandad found in the box explained what had happened to the ship and what they had discovered."

"Who discovered?" Alice asks leaning in closer.

"The note explained how two fishermen named William Thomas and Tristan Richards found the shipwreck in 1789. They found treasure where the remains of the ship lay."

Alice reaches out and holds my hand and says, "Tim, your surname is Richards."

"Tristan was my relation, he was family." I respond, the connection sending shivers down my spine.

"So why are we here now with this map?" She asks.

"Well, there's a ship out there with gold and jewels and maybe much more. We know it's out there. We have a written account and a map that proves it."

"That still doesn't explain why we're looking at the map now," She presses.

"A salvage company has information regarding the Spanish ship, our ship, and plans to explore this area at the end of the year. As soon as we heard this news,

Grandad and I agreed that it's worth one more shot. It took a little persuasion, well not too much actually, but Grandad has agreed to look for the treasure one more time. We plan on diving again" I say.

"Even after you lost your Dad doing exactly that, you feel you want to try again?"

"That's what makes it even more important," I say. "This map has been in the family for years, and it feels as though it was always meant to be ours."

"I get it! So, what next?"

"Grandad and I have agreed to try again, but we need help."

"So, you want me to help you Tim?" Alice asks.

"Yeah, you and a few others."

"Count me in! What an adventure. How bloody exciting!" her enthusiasm is infectious.

We both stand, the ocean stretching out before us, a vast expanse of dark blue rippling under the pale light of the sky. The waves crash against the rocks, with a wild sound that mirrors the emotions within me.

Alice looks over, a newfound determination in her eyes. "Who else knows? Who else is going to be involved? Who can we trust?"

Chapter 11
Recruitment begins

I have to bang hard on Dylan's door as he's usually playing his music loud or busy in the kitchen. Alice, standing by my side, sniffs the air and looks over at me with a knowing smile. Dylan opens the door wearing what can only be described as a very tight pair of jeggings and no top. Dylan buys most of his clothes from local charity shops, and I'm sure he gets a bit confused with what he's actually buying. For some reason, it really doesn't matter - he manages to pull off most things with his own quirky vibe. He once turned up at my house wearing a long sheepskin Afghan-style coat with a black denim kilt and Dr Marten boots. Hippy meets rock star legend springs to mind. Dylan's fashion sense is as eclectic as it is unpredictable.

"Dydh da," he says, leaning straight in giving Alice a massive cuddle and kissing her on the cheek. A flirt and a charmer, is Dylan. He looks over to me and winks. "Come in, come in, coffee?"

Dylan's home has its own unique smell. It's a combination of incense, weed, and home cooking. Dylan leads the way through to the kitchen, which is at the back of the house. The kitchen's a random mix of antiques, crafts, and driftwood furniture that he's made over the years. Dylan's a great cook and always has something prepared or in the oven. Just our luck, freshly made bread is sitting, waiting to be eaten.

"What brings you lovers 'round here?" Dylan sits cross-legged in a deep kitchen window seat, surrounded by all sorts of house plants. He prepares a joint while ordering me to make the coffee and slice the bread.

"Use the fresh organic butter dude" He demands.

Alice is glancing around the kitchen at what can only be described as a haven for all things foody. There're cookery books on shelves, jars with every herb known to man, dried stuff, berries, and nuts. Kitchen utensils are hanging from the ceiling and a large, hand-built wooden table is the kitchen's centrepiece.

"We've a proposition for you, but it's to be kept a complete secret. If you say yes, know this Dylan: you must promise never to speak about this to anyone." Dylan looks directly at me with intrigue. He licks his long Rizla paper in one fluid motion, lights his joint, and with a fresh cloud of smoke creating a silhouette around him, looks up almost in slow motion and says, "I'm in!"

Alice replies, "Don't you want to know what we're about to ask of you before you commit?"

"For sure, but I've known this lad since he was about six, and if he's up to something, then I'm always gunna be a part of it, no doubting that."

We start from the beginning and tell Dylan everything. Dylan, fixated on all the details as I knew he would be, listens intently. You could see him processing everything much like a computer collecting data. Several cups of coffee and one loaf of fresh bread demolished, we sit in silence, looking at each other. Dylan takes a deep breath, "Well, that's a lot of information my lovers. How sure are you there's actually treasure on this wreck? Other than the story, the map, and the old Spanish carved box, what else do we have to go on?"

"Dylan, until we go down, we'll never know, but if it is down there, then this is an opportunity to change lives and make a difference to our community," Alice adds.

"So, what part do you want me to play?" Dylan asks.

"Diving," I reply.

"Diving? I've not dived for flipping years. I'm rusty dude."

"That's fine," Alice replies, "we have the perfect place to practise."

"What about you Tim? Sam's spilled the beans about your secret little swimming lessons you twat. Surely you're not diving?"

Alice comments "Don't you worry; I'll bring him up to speed. Your role will be to plan, ensure that we get everything right, no surprises. Detail Dylan, attention to detail - that's your role in all this mate."

Dylan continues, "So, it's us three, who else has

agreed to be part of this crazy treasure-hunting experience?"

"Grandad and Max, the old boys." I reply.

"What the fuck?" Dylan buries his head in his hands. "Dude you know this whole thing's fucked with those two looneys involved."

You sure you've thought this through bro? Bloody Grandad, you know he keeps popping round asking for joints?"

"Yeah I know, just pretend you're out next time."

"He peers through the window though dude, it's weird. Anyone else?"

*

The sun is breaking through to reveal a stunning Cornish day. Sam's putting out the weathered benches as Alice and I walk towards the café.

"Wasson you two? fancy helping with the food preparation? Daisy's stressed right out, that new lad hasn't shown up again. He's gone AWOL. I told Daisy he's gunna be an unreliable one, but what do I know?" he mutters. "On one condition," I say. "We'll help if you agree to join us tonight down at Bottom Beach for some food and a late-night swim."

"Oh, you're a swimmer now then?" Sam laughs. "Proper Cornish you've become, you'll be eating pasties next. Ok you're on," he flings over aprons for us both, then shouts out to Daisy, "The cavalry's here!" Daisy quickly puts us to work whilst looking me straight in the eyes and says in a firm, schoolteacher-like tone, "Don't eat any of the food, got it?"

"Would I?" She pushes me, demanding we get to work.

*

That night, there's a calm, golden glow across the sandy beach. The sun, now a fiery orb nearing the horizon, paints the sky with hues of orange and a unique pinkish red. A gentle breeze carries the invigorating scent of the sea. The all-familiar rhythmic melody of the ocean waves soothingly plays in the background. Sam, ever the barbecue head chef, stands cooking on the open flame. The barbecues dancing smoke moves in every direction on an ever-changing sea breeze. Daisy and Alice are stood at the water's edge barefoot, looking out into the distance.

After dinner and with the light of day fading, it's time to ask our trusted friends if they wanted to become part of an adventure that could change their lives forever.

"What's on your mind then bro?" asks Sam. "I can sense you've got something in that head of yours; you've been distracted the whole night." The four of us sit together around the fire. Alice and I start to reveal the story so far. Both Sam and Daisy are silent, listening intently.

After some time walking them through all the information. Alice asks. "So, a question for you both, are you in? Do you fancy being part of this crazy treasure-hunting adventure?"

"What part do you want us to play?" Sam asks.

"How's your diving skills?" Alice responds, her voice bright and teasing, as if inviting the thrill of adventure into the air around us.

Both Sam and Daisy exchange a glance, a spark of mischief igniting between them. In an instant, they break into a high five. "That's what we're talking about!" their eyes gleaming with excitement.

"We're going to need a little practice time, haven't done much diving for a few years eh Sam?" Daisy leans in closer, her voice lowering. "But hell yeah, I'm so excited to be heading back down to the depths of the sea again. I'm not sure about seaweed though, freaks me out a bit not gunna lie."

"So, you're both in?"

"Never a doubt my old friend, never a doubt. Who else knows about this?" Sam asks.

"Grandad and Max."

"So, the two oldies, us four, anyone else?"

"One more," I say.

"Hold on, not Dylan?" Sam looks concerned. "What part is the stoner playing?"

"Dylan's our problem solver, you know how he loves

to plan. He thinks about every little detail, we need him to focus on planning, we can't afford for anything to go wrong. Alice and I will also be diving. So that's it, that's our motley crew."

"We'll need a boat and diving equipment."

I reply, "What do you think we've enlisted the old pirate for."

Sam, with a nod in my direction, questions, "Will he be ready?"

"I'll get him ready," Alice responds. "We have access to a swimming pool where we can practise before we can issue your diving licences. I'm not gunna just dish them out, you'll have to work hard for them."

Sam looks at Alice. "So, you're doing this properly then, proper licences and all that? When's the dive happening then people?".

"One month," both Alice and I confirm together.

"Hold on, one month? How the bloody hell do we get ready in just one month?" Sam looks stunned and overwhelmed, not his normal carefree self.

"We start tomorrow," Alice confirms.

"Shit," says Daisy. "You're both off your heads, but I love it."

"One other question I've got for you both. Before we fully commit to this crazy-ass plan of yours, if we manage to pull this off and there's treasure down there, what then? What's the split? How do we turn treasure into money? We can't pop down the local and buy our weekly shop with some golden cups or some precious jewels."

"We need to find the stuff first! But for now, a toast to friendship and our crazy ass adventure." We raise our drinks and continue into the night talking and planning.

Chapter 12

Preparation is key

Alice and I park by the swimming pool, the old boys are unloading the diving equipment, Dylan's just behind us, but there's no sign of Sam and Daisy yet. We gather the equipment and head in. The old boys, along with Alice, are preparing while Dylan and I sit on the side, talking through our plans.

I hear a flop, flop sound and look up to see Sam with an audacious grin on his face. Confidently, he struts in from behind the changing room area, donned in a vibrant collection of eccentric swim gear, including a bright orange rubber ring, arm bands, flippers, snug speedos, and a snorkel perched on his face. Everyone stops what they're doing and stares at this aquatic spectacle before their eyes. Laughter erupts, echoing around the pool. Sam's rubber ring squeaks with each step he takes, and the flippers make a comical slapping sound against the pool's tiles. He walks with an air of elegance and steps off the edge into the water with a graceful descent. Bobbing up and down, he shouts out, "Ready? Let's do this treasure hunting thing!" Laughter continues.

Dylan walks over to Grandad and jokingly asks "You're not diving then Grandad? You have your own natural buoyance aid right there in front of you," Dylan laughs whilst slapping Grandads belly. "Piss off hippy."

With an air of excitement mixed with nerves, Alice and Max guide me through the process, adjusting our masks and checking our oxygen tanks, while the others reacquaint themselves. We work on embracing buoyancy and weightlessness. The night is a success, with careful control and guidance from them both. To think it's not that long ago I couldn't even swim, and now I'm learning how to dive! I'm chuffed with the progress I've made and so excited for what's to come.

We agree to meet again at the end of the week to keep practising. "We need to work on hand gestures and feel confident that we can all communicate well together underwater. It's so important that above all, we're looking out for each other ensuring that we're safe at all times." Alice points out, "Remember, I'll need to see you perform at five dives in open water, and you have to take the theory test before I can issue you all with your licences. Jim and I won't issue any licences unless we are completely happy with your progress. There's no diving without a licence, and you only have three weeks to convince me, so there's a lot of work to do."

*

That night, after diving practice, Grandad, Alice, and I sit in the kitchen. Grandad is sitting quietly and hasn't joined the conversation for a while, "You okay Grandad?" I ask. He looks up at us both. I can see the worry on his face; his eyes are still and sad, his expression, one of concern.

"I am, thanks Tim, I just can't help the feelings this is bringing back to me. Yer Dad and I saw the whole thing as such an adventure all those years ago, jus' as yew all do now. Although I feel excited again, I'm also terrified about losing yew, any of yew, for tha' matter. I've never healed from the sorrow of losing yer Dad. I've buried tha' pain the best I could, but if I'm honest, I'm struggling with it all at the moment."

"Grandad talk to us, it's okay to talk." Grandad looks down towards the table, avoiding eye contact. Running his old, weathered finger around, following the natural grain of the wood repeatedly, almost trance-like, he begins sharing the memories of that day.

"I can remember sitting on the boat jus' waiting for him to come back. I felt so alone. I kept looking at my watch and saying, jus' a couple more minutes. Ee didn't come back. Minutes became an hour. I waited and waited, looking for any signs. My mind and the sea began to trick me as I scanned the horizon, bubbles and movements captured my attention, I was sure it was him returning. Pacing up and down until suddenly, I felt it in the pit of my stomach. I knew, right then, I jus' knew."

As Grandad is telling us about that day, my chest tightens with fear, and a coldness comes over me, my mouth's dry, and anxiety rushes through my whole body. I feel as if I am there on the boat with him, sharing the pain. I look over at Alice. A blankness on her face captured by Grandad's tone, his voice quivering, and cracking with emotion.

"Making tha' decision to leave and come home was the 'ardest decision I've ever had to make in my life. I tried to leave several times, starting the boat and then shuttin' it down again." He looks up, "I really don't think I could go through tha' loss again." Grandad's eyes so sad and sunken.

We all take a moment with our own personal thoughts.

"This time it will be different Grandad, Dad dived alone, and that presented its own risks. We'll be diving together, allowing us to keep an eye on each other. Alice will not let any of us dive if she's not one hundred percent happy, will you Alice?"

Alice looks at Grandad, "This must be really difficult for you, stirring up so many memories." Grandad responds, "Promise me this, only dive if yew feel ready and abandon the dive if something's not right. Promise me yew will both look out for each other and the others."

Alice reaches out and holds Grandad's hand. "I promise not to take any unnecessary risks. The dive will only happen if I'm completely sure it is safe to do so."

*

I lie in bed, staring at the ceiling, thinking through

the conversation we shared that evening. It's late, and sleep evades me. My mind becomes restless, thoughts and doubts creeping in like shadows at the edges of my consciousness. Are we gambling with our lives in pursuit of this treasure? Has this become reckless?

This treasure has been consuming my every waking moment, it's felt like destiny - our destiny. It is ours, isn't it? Dad started this, and I had vowed to finish it in his name. But now... now, I'm not so sure. I'm asking so much of the people I love. I'm asking them to risk everything for me and the treasure. Am I about to lose even more people I love for something that might not even exist?

Frustration boils inside me, I toss and turn, unable to silence the gnawing doubts flashing through my mind.

The night stretches on endlessly. My gaze locks onto a thin sliver of moonlight creeping through the window. I focus on the light and my mind begins to quiet, as I drift towards sleep... The sliver of light now above me, guides me down to the wreck like a torch. It's there, I can see it just beyond the darkness, waiting for me. A coldness, unnatural and suffocating, seeps into my bones. I look up - the light, my only tether to safety, is slipping away. The further I go, the darker it gets. Everything looks the same, I'm confused, disoriented, it's so dark. I've been down here too long. I'm scared. My chest tightens, constricting painfully. I'm running out of air. Panic strikes, sharp and sudden, like a blade to my gut, my breathing quickens; inhale, exhale, inhale, exhale, faster, faster, faster - I'm hyperventilating. I fumble with my oxygen gauge, there's almost nothing left. A cold, choking terror wraps around me. My heart pounds against my ribcage as my mind races. Will I have enough oxygen to make it back to the surface?

I have to ascend. Now.

I'm desperate to rise, but my limbs are sluggish, as if weighted down by the freezing water. The cold is unbearable, numbing me, stealing the strength from my muscles. *I'm so cold.* Where's the boat? I should see it by now. But it's gone. The boat... it's gone. I've drifted too far, too far from safety. Frantic, I thrash through the water, heading in the direction I think the boat should be. But there's nothing. No sign of it. Where is it? Where's the *fucking* boat? I break through the surface of the water, gasping for air as I pull off my mask but I'm alone and there's no boat. The ocean stretches out in every direction, an endless, freezing expanse. No boat. No land. Just me, adrift, lost in the darkness. The cold seeps into my core, an icy grip tightening around my heart, my muscles tremble, weak and exhausted, and my thoughts begin to blur. I just need to close my eyes. Just for a moment. I just need to rest, go to sleep and rest.

One last breath.

I jolt awake, sitting bolt upright in bed, my lungs burning and I'm drenched in sweat, yet freezing cold. I blink, disoriented, struggling to pull myself back to reality.

It was a dream. Just a dream. I'm okay.

But as I sit there, gasping for breath, I can still

feel it - the icy grip of terror, the weight of the water dragging me down. My hands tremble as I force myself to breathe, each inhale shaky and ragged. "Relax," I whisper to myself, trying to push the fear away. "It was only a dream." But the dream clings to me, refusing to let go. Vivid and haunting, it lingers at the edges of my mind. I can still feel the terror, the disorientation and the cold. It felt so real, like I've just lived Dad's last moments; lost, scared, confused, and utterly alone, and there was no boat?

I rest my head back onto the damp pillow and search for peace.

*

The next three weeks are spent practising building confidence in our diving. We complete the theory test and are on our last day of open sea practice. Moments of my dream come and go, I've questioned everything since. The dream now more vague, unclear, but I can't shake the memory of there being no boat when I came up.

It's our final practise dive and Alice informs us, "The water is choppy today, be aware of the ocean and its movements. Be aware of the underwater currents and tidal swells; they may present some challenges. I want us all back safely in thirty minutes. This is the deepest we've been to date; it'll be a good test for us all." Alice confirms the importance of working as a team and using all the hand gestures we'd been practicing.

The initial plunge feels like a deliberate surrender to the unknown, immersed in a world that echoes with the rhythmic pulsing of the ocean. As we descend, the pressure gently embraces us, the water transforming from turquoise to sapphire, and finally to deep inky blue. Sunlight filters through, creating ethereal shafts of light that dance between us. Schools of fish swirl around, fascinated by our arrival. Alice, leading the way, points her thumb down to indicate the intention to descend further. The five of us are now working as a sequenced team with roles that have naturally developed. Sam, the timekeeper, hand signals how long we have been down. The water becomes darker with a denser feeling than our previous dives; as this is the deepest dive so far, it certainly feels different. Alice was right, there are stronger undercurrents. As we make our way deeper, I find the darkness strangely comforting, a sanctuary where time seems to stand still and the worries of the world fall into insignificance. Alice signals with a thumb up that it's time to ascend.

*

That night, we all head to Sam's café for our final meeting before the dive. It is so important that every detail is covered. The rich aroma of coffee lingers from the day's trading. In the dimly lit ambience of Sam's café, candles flicker whilst generations come together. I sit back to appreciate the moment, watching young and old interact with one common purpose. Age seems to separate people, which I've often thought a shame.

If only we spent more time together, we would learn so much more from each other.

Dylan's rolled a couple of joints and places them on the table. Max's hand reaches into a knitted bag, revealing a bottle of rum, his expression one of an excited child. With the map carefully spread across the table we delve into the final plans. The old boys, grizzled by time, exchange knowing glances and banter with each other. Excitement resonates in all of our voices at the adventure that lies ahead, all eyes gleaming with the prospect of discovering hidden treasures beneath the ocean's surface. Yet amid the thrill and excitement, the dream has added a new layer of doubts. Concern for our safety and the weight of uncertainty is heavy for me to bear.

Max pours the aged rum which cascades into the waiting glass, a rich and evocative aroma unfurling, Sam reaches for a glass, "I think I'll join you". Max passes him the bottle. Alice leans over towards Dylan and picks up a joint. The potent smell blends with the rum, weaving a tapestry of scents. Dylan smiles as Alice sits back in her chair with a new sense of ease and calmness. Laughter flows, mingled with genuine appreciation and moments of silence while the rum and joints do their rounds.

Max stands up, glass in hand, and says, "I wanna make a toast." Grandad taps his glass to usher in silence. "May this adventure bring us success in wha' we seek, but above all, may the ocean keep us safe."

Alice is next up. "I have a new family here now, and I love you all." She leans over to me and says,

"Especially you Beach Boy," and kisses me. A cheer and clapping follow. Grandad slaps me on the back with a lovely smile, "Beach Boy," he laughs. The group leans into the middle of the table and clinks glasses. Sam announces, "Here's to our new family, and here's to finding that bloody treasure lads!"

Daisy heads towards the café's sound system, suddenly "Movin' on Up" fills the space. Everyone gets to their feet and starts dancing in their own way. The night continues as you would expect, fuelled by our new sense of family.

Chapter 13

Dive day

With the preparation's done, the diving certificates granted, the plan completed in great detail and Max's boat fully equipped, we leave the safety of the harbour at first light. The conditions are on our side, proving favourable with just gentle swells. The sky stretches above us, reaching out to the far-off horizon as the boat slices through the sea, leaving a trail of white froth in its wake. The rhythmic chug of the engine echoes across the water, mingling with the cries of gulls as they circle above. The air's thick with tension, a palpable mix of excitement and anticipation, like a living entity, pulsating with every ripple on the water's surface, and with every creak of the vessel. We all exchange glances on and off, as if to reassure each other - a silent affirmation of the shared fears and anxieties that have been gently wrapped with hope.

"A great day to find tha' therr treasure!" Max shouts out.

I sit with Grandad, who's looking into the distance. I

lean over and wrap my arm around his shoulder, knowing that he's fearful, apprehensive, and full of memories from the past. "It will be fine," I say. He looks back into my eyes, "I hope so son," slowly he returns his gaze to the open sea and beyond. Alice is sitting with Dylan, going through some final checks of the plan, Sam and Daisy are checking equipment.

I approach Alice from behind and enclose my arms around her, squeezing gently. "You take care out there today mind," I whisper. She turns to face me, her eyes reflecting the inky tone of the blue that surrounds us, her lips brush against mine. The kiss gentle, yet filled with unspoken intensity.

We arrive at where we believe the shipwreck is located, some distance away from the original dive site where Grandad and Dad had tried so many years ago. I grab the original map, and we huddle around it, looking deep into the etched details, hoping that we have the right spot. Sam and Daisy are putting on their wetsuits as it's been agreed they will do a pre-dive to explore the site. Max turns off the engine. The boat settles and gently rocks as the anchor descends into the depths. Both Sam and Daisy sit on the edge of the boat, preparing for the first dive down.

"Good luck guys."

"Remember, safety always," Dylan adds.

With a resolute nod, they both execute a graceful backward roll into the sea with barely a splash, fins slicing through the water as their silhouettes slowly fade. The surface ripples subside, replaced by bubbles, leaving a pristine canvas of blues and whites. Grandad nervously starts to pace around the boat as Dylan and I lean over the side, peering deep into the darkness with eagerness.

Twenty minutes pass, and the first signs of Sam and Daisy returning become visible. The hiss of air from the regulator and the rhythmic hum of bubbles amplified as they slowly return to the surface. We all gather with anticipation, and then help them back on deck, where Sam pulls off his mask and looks straight at me.

"Nothing Tim. Nothing down there." Sam's face is full of disappointment.

We all agree to move slightly farther out and dive again. This time, it's just Alice and me, tasked with scoping the area. With wetsuits zipped up and equipment double-checked, we slide into the water. The cold instantly grips me. Together, we descend, the surface above us dissolving into rippling silver as the ocean closes in around us.

The deeper we go, the darker it becomes. Shafts of muted sunlight struggle to pierce the water, replaced by an eerie, shadowy gloom. I notice that my breathing sounds louder through the regulator, each inhale and exhale seem more predominate then before. I feel different this time, and I'm struggling to shake the unease that's creeping in.

A knot of anxiety begins to form in my stomach, coiling tighter with every meter we descend. I glance at Alice, her silhouette moving methodically, scanning the seabed with practiced and precise sweeps. The glow of her light cuts through the darkness, but it does little to calm me. I see her focus and confidence, yet it makes my own doubt sharper for some reason. Suddenly, the memory of the dream resurfaces; disjointed and haunting. I see us drifting, lost and swallowed by the endless void of the ocean.

My pulse quickens, and I feel the first wave of panic set in. What if we drift too far? What if we lose each other? What if we lose the boat? The questions spiral, and my breath grows faster, harsher. The regulator feels intrusive now, each inhalation too shallow and each exhalation rushed. I try to steady myself, gripping the strap of my diving gear as if it might anchor me to a sense of safety. Calm, *Tim just remain calm, you must relax.* Is all I keep repeating over and over again.

Alice's light flashes towards me, snapping me back to reality. Her hand signals for calm, her gestures deliberate and soothing. She's noticed my hesitation. Her eyes meet mine through her mask, and even in the murky water, I can feel her looking into my soul. I nod, confirming I was ok to continue. She stares at me as if she wasn't convinced. We take a moment and then move forward.

We search tirelessly, the beams of our lights piercing the water but revealing only sand, rocks, and strands of seaweed swaying like ghostly figures. The emptiness around us feels vast, and doubt begins to creep in again. Is this shipwreck truly here? Alice signals time and together we slowly head back to the surface. The first thing I see is the boat and Grandad peering over, much to my relief.

"How did you get on" Dylan asks. I'm hesitant with my words and try hard not to show I had struggled with this dive. Alice confirms nothing down there. I glance around, only to see disappointed faces. Only adding to the weight of the panic and doubts creeping in from the haunting return of the dream. Sam instantly questions the whole situation, "Well perhaps this is just a story after all?" Max makes his way to the edge of the boat. He scans the horizon before turning to face us all. "Look at the vastness of this ocean, if she's down therr she ain't gunna make it easy for us but I'm fucked if we're giving up now, not after we've done all this work. "We just need to reference all of this area." Dylan says, as he joins Max looking out to sea. "We need to sweep an area at a time, carefully moving out in different directions. We can create a grid system; assigning each section a reference number or letter to ensure no spot is disregarded. If it's down there, we'll bloody find it."

As everyone is discussing a plan for a grid system, Alice approaches me. She has a worried expression and I think I know why. "We need to talk, not now but we definitely need to talk."

Max starts up the boat as Grandad pulls up the anchor and we start heading back towards the harbour. Everyone is quietly lost in their own thoughts and Alice's comment is all I can think about. I don't know what came over me down there, but she knows. Alice saw my distress and unease that's for sure.

Reaching the safety of the harbour, we say our goodbyes and go our separate ways. However, Alice and I hang back on the boat. "What happened down there today Beach Boy? You lost your focus, you were not in the moment, it was clear to see. I can't have you diving if you're a risk to yourself and to the others."

With a deep sigh, I slump back onto the bench seat. "A few months ago, I had a dream, more like a nightmare. I was diving alone and I was lost, it was as if I was living Dads diving experience. In the dream, I felt the emotions that he must have felt running through me. When I finally returned to the surface, there was no boat. The boat had gone and I was alone, floating, stranded, cold and confused. I took my last breath and suddenly I woke up shivering. The dream has stayed with me. I thought that I had processed it and I had it under control, but then whilst diving today, out of nowhere, terror and a sense of panic flooded my mind. I struggled to remain calm, I'm so sorry."

"It's not about being sorry, it's about safety. My job is to keep you all safe and that's a big responsibility. I'm pulling you out of the next dive. You need to take some time and make sure that you have properly worked through this. This cannot happen again Tim."

*

Two weeks pass and several dives later, there is still no sign of the shipwreck. I've not dived again, but I feel that I've made progress on processing the apprehension attached to the dream. I think I'm ready to go back down.

Dylan has been mapping out the area and his gridding system is progressing the search. He's pinned a few different sites on the map that could be where the shipwreck lies and today we're heading to a spot slightly west of where we first dived. As we approach the area, Alice and Dylan prepare to dive. The sun's bouncing off the swell, and an inner warmth consumes me.

Alice returns first, breaking through the swell. She has something in her hand, an object of some sort. Dylan follows and excitedly pulls off his mask, shouting, "It's there! It's bloody right there!" He slaps the water with excitement. Alice's hand stretches out, and I grab the object. We help them both back onto the boat. Max runs over full of questions. Grandad and Sam start swinging each other around, laughing like a pair of excitable children.

We gather round Alice as she starts to fill us in with the details. "It's a wreck, but it seems small, smaller than I would have thought. I'm not sure it's our wreck. This is definitely a spot we need to explore though."

I study Alice's object, it's an intricately painted tile, faded over years. Dylan takes the tile and gently starts cleaning it, before grabbing his phone and searching for a reference. He finds a Spanish design that is so similar *it can't be a coincidence.* The atmosphere on the boat is electric, and everyone is busy preparing for the next dive while looking at each other with camaraderie.

"It's so dark down there. Our lights might not be enough," Alice says. "We will all need as much light as possible." Max opens up one of the boxes at the rear of the boat and pulls out a large LED light. "This should do the job." We all get ready to dive together. "Good luck everyone." Daisy says, as she pulls us in for a group hug.

Alice pulls me to one side and asks, "You ok? You ready?"

"I'm fine honestly, I'm ready."

"At any stage, if you have a moment, I would prefer you to return with no hesitation. We can't risk it Tim."

"I will, I promise."

Slowly, we make our way down, Alice leading and Dylan as always, at the rear of the group. The natural light of the world we're leaving behind fades, and the darkness of our new realm becomes ever more prominent. In the murkiness and in ghostly silence, the shipwreck gradually materializes as if it were moving towards us in slow motion. Our flashlights highlight the timeworn remnants, the ship's skeletal frame stands frozen, an eerie testament to the passage of time. Truly beautiful is the sight. As we approach the wreck, our torches illuminate patches with an ethereal glow. The light sweeps across it and highlights the details of the wood. The grain of the timber, once polished and strong, is now coarse, dark, almost blackened brown, rough and etched by the corrosive touch of saltwater.

I swim over to Sam, and together we head to what looks like the stern of the ship. Sam points two fingers at his eyes and then to a large cannon that has found its final resting place. The once-imposing weapon is now softened by time, its edges rounded and smoothed by the constant caress of the undercurrents. Alice and Daisy head further along the seabed into the distance. Here and there, colours catch the eye; tiny, iridescent fish darting in and out of the crevices, their scales reflecting the torchlight in shimmering rainbows. The play of light and shadow creates a mesmerising dance on the wooden surfaces, with the beams highlighting the curves and contours of the ship's damaged remains, casting long, eerie shadows that stretch into the unseen corners of the deep.

The seabed, adorned with silt and sediment, cradles the shipwreck. With every movement, fine particles swirl around us. The silt, ranging from fine, almost invisible grains to larger, more noticeable flecks, appears to move in slow motion. Each particle glints like a microscopic diamond, creating tiny flashes of light that seem to hang in the water, suspended in time. We slowly and carefully move into the core of the wreck's body.

Dylan; taps me on the back and points to where Alice and Daisy have gone, signalling to follow. As we arrive, Alice is pointing downwards using her beam, moving it from side to side. It's not clear what she's trying to show us, but a faint glistening catches our attention as the beam passes over it. Alice uses her hands in a slow sweeping motion to disperse the age-old silt, and to our amazement, gold and silver coins appear. Fist pumps confirm the sense of overwhelming excitement as we set eyes on treasure for the very first time. Between us, we gather the coins and put them in our bags. To the far left of the group, Daisy's now gently moving a worn piece of wood to access the remains of boxes encrusted with barnacles. Around the boxes are what look like eroded cloth bags, delicate and worn from years of resting at the bottom of the deep ocean. As she touches the cloth bags, they disintegrate as if they were vanishing before our eyes and particles of perished material merge with the silt. The specks slowly settle, revealing what had been hidden away for so many years. A cascade of gems, jewels, precious stones, gold, and silver spills forth, catching the refracted light like a submerged constellation. The sea seems to shimmer in response, as if it self is rejoicing at the revelation. Dylan appears and signals "Time," pointing up for us to return. We gather what we have found, carefully adding the treasure to our collection bags. One by one, drifting slowly in and out of darkness and light we make our way back to the boat. As I remove my mask, I look around and panic for one second as Dylan has not yet appeared. Bubbles and swirls then break through the surface's membrane. A sigh of relief as we've all made it back, followed by a rush of excitement for what we've discovered. Soon, we all realise the enormity of our findings and quickly begin to reveal to each other the contents of our collection bags. I look up to see Grandad crying, whilst Sam's just staring at it all.

"We've done it!" I shout. "We've fucking done it!"

Momentarily frozen in time, we exchange wide-eyed glances as we realise the magnitude of our discovery: gleaming jewels, emeralds, rubies, gold, and silver. Unable to contain our joy, cheers and laughter seem to echo across the waves, bouncing off the cliffs as if it were just us in this moment, where the present has intertwined with the past and nobody knows.

"We're diving again, right?" asks Sam. "We have to," replies Daisy. "We didn't clear the area, and I am sure there's still more down there. We can't leave it behind, not now." We agree on one more dive.

Chapter 14

We dive again

Together, we head back down. Daisy and I reach the spot where we'd found the precious stones and we begin to investigate the area further, gently moving our hands to disperse the silt and sand. Daisy points at what looks like muskets lodged within the seabed. We move along a little further, within the debris are boxes similar in size to the one Grandad has, so I move some crusted wood to gain access. Sparkling in the brightness from the beams of our lights, more treasure is revealed. The reflected colours are captivating, we gather all we can find.

Alice and Sam have made their way to the central area of the wreck, and we head over to join them. As we arrive, they're trying to move a large wooden beam covered in algae, wedged between rocks and what looks like some rigging; the beam solid, dark with age. Together we manage to slowly move it just enough for Alice to swim under. There in all its glory, is a collection of golden bars, pendants and large chains are scattered across the seabed. Alice adds them to her collection bag. Suddenly, an ominous deep creaking sound echoes through the still water. The beam shifts unexpectedly, dislodging from its precarious position. Before anyone can react, the beam's pinned Alice's leg underneath, trapping her. Immediately hysteria sets in. A silent scream escapes her as she thrashes, trying to free herself.

I signal frantically to Dylan for help! Extending my hand out flat as I wobble it side to side. Our careful coordinated movements now chaotic and desperate.

Alice's eyes look deeply into mine, filled with distress. Seeing her so vulnerable threatens to overwhelm me. Her breathing becomes rapid, sharp bursts release bubbles that race towards the surface. Dylan joins Sam and me grabbing one end of the beam, trying to lift it whilst Daisy works to free Alice's leg. The beam's heavy and our efforts ineffective, we reposition ourselves and try again. My muscles tremble as exhaustion hits me quicker than expected. The water around us, churns with clouds of silt and sand, blurring our vision, hindering our attempts and Alice fades into the murkiness. Working together we manage to lift it ever so slightly, just enough to pull Alice's leg free. Daisy slides Alice from the beam's clutches. Dylan franticly gestures a flat hand movement across his throat, indicating we're running low on air and we need to return.

As we start to make our ascent, not knowing the extent of her injuries, every second feels like an eternity. The darkness slowly gives way to the light. Finally, we break through the water's surface.

I quickly remove my mask and shout out. "Grandad, help Alice!" He grabs her arm and together we carefully help her back onto the boat. "What's happened?"

"She got her leg trapped under a beam." Alice's face is pale, her body trembling from the ordeal. "You ok love? how's your leg?"

"I'm fine," her voice shaky and weak. "Can you move your leg?" Grandad asks. "It's ok, the beam just trapped me; my leg feels fine. I was so scared; I didn't think I was going to make it." Dylan, seeing Alice trembling, asks, "Do you want us to take you to the hospital, get you checked over?"

"Honestly my leg's fine, nothing's broken. I'm just glad to be back on this boat."

"Let's get you out of that suit and into some dry clothes." I cuddle and pull her in tight for warmth. Max fires up the boat, a plume of dark smoke fills the air and we slowly head back in the direction of land. I sit and stare at Alice, the reality of nearly losing her down there just confirms how much I need her in my life.

Now,

Choose which ending you wish to read.

Read on from here for the happy ending.

 Or skip to life's complicated alternative ending.

My advice, read both!

Chapter 15

The realisation

The sun's dipping below the horizon and the first stars are emerging as we return, a mix of emotions from the day's events is clear on everyone's faces. We arrive back at the boatyard relieved; we're all safe, and so excited about what we've discovered.

The large wooden door creaks as Max gives it a firm shove and walks into the darkness of the office. He snaps the lights on, the fluorescent bulbs flicker into action. Max disappears for a moment, returning with a large bottle of rum and a selection of mismatched mugs.

"A toast!" he bellows, his voice booming above the laughter and chatter that's now filling the room. As Max pours slugs of rum, Dylan clears a space on the large rustic wooden table, and carefully we place the treasure into the middle. Glimmering under the light, as we gather around mesmerised by its beauty, it seems proud to be seen once again.

Sam breaks the silence "What the hell do we do now,

look at it all? More importantly, where are we selling ancient, precious jewels? Can't sell this sort of shit at a car boot sale." A few nervous chuckles ripple through the room, but the question hangs in the air with the uncertainty it brings, twisting the excitement into something more complex. The reality of the treasure, and its implications, begins to settle in.

Max and Grandad, oblivious to what happens next, are lighting cigars and pouring their second mugs of rum, laughing and slapping each other on the back in a congratulatory manner. I watch Alice walk to the door.

Outside, she's staring up into the night sky. "The stars are bright tonight," she says as I walk behind her and wrap my arms around her waist, gently kissing her on the neck. I ask, "How's your leg feeling now?"

"I thought I was going to die today, I was so scared. In that moment all I could think about was you. You're the one."

"The one?" I ask. "The one that's captured my heart." Alice takes a deep breath, her voice now a gentle melody in the stillness. "You've captured my heart, Beach Boy."

The night seems to hold its breath, as if the world itself paused to witness this moment. "Ever since we sat on my longboard and you nearly drowned, I've been slowly falling in love with you, I've tried not to, but it's impossible. You've shown me you, it's as if I've known you forever."

Alice cups my face with her soft, warm hands, her eyes glistening with sincerity. The gentle breeze of the night sweeps strands of her hair across her face. She slowly leans forward and kisses me. "How lucky are we? out of all the people in the world, it's you." We collapse into each other, laughing. I shout out, "What a day to be alive! What a fucking day." That feeling, the profound sense of comfort, being accepted for who you truly are. It's a warmth that wraps around the heart, what words can explain love? You just feel it pulsing deep within.

As we re – enter Sam leaps forward and with a very excited expression announces. "I think I may know someone that might be able to help with this lot." Daisy looks confused as she asks "Who's that Sam?"

"Allan"

"Which Allan?"

"Dodgy Allan."

"Great, I don't like the sound of this straight away. Who has a mate called Dodgy Allan?" Replies Alice. "He does, by the sound of it." Dylan says, nodding towards Sam. "What? Allan, who got you the TV?" Questions Daisy. "Yeah, he knows people and if anyone can get rid of this treasure, Allan can." Responds Sam. Dylan gets up, shaking his head, not at all convinced with Sam's plan. "I'm off for a rolly." As he walks past Sam laughing, he slaps him round the head and says under his breath, "Dodgy Allan! What the fuck Sam?" Sam replies with, "Honestly, it's the best shout we have at the moment guys. It's worth reaching out to him at the very least, what have we got to lose? Unless anyone else has a better idea?" From the distance, Dylan shouts back, "Shit loads of treasure Sam, that's what we have to lose mate!"

Grandad joins the conversation, "Nobody with the name dodgy Allan is gunna be trust worthy, tha's for sure. How do yew know this bloke anyway?" Daisy looks over at Sam and starts to reveal their back story. "He met him at a car boot sale years ago and bought a TV from him. They've been buddy's ever since and have done many a dodgy deal. Hence the name dodgy Allan! But I like him, I think he's really funny." Now catching Grandads eye, "You know our sound system in the café? That came from dodgy Allan!" Sam chimes in and proudly says, with a slight shoulder shrug, "And it's brilliant, that sound system, isn't it? Let's at least make contact. We don't have to give him too much information. We can say we have inherited some gems and jewels? Find out if he can move it on or if he knows someone who's in the market to buy this sort of thing."

Dylan calls from outside, "This is a shit idea you lot! Let it be known that I'm not happy." Max, sitting in the armchair, leans forward and says, "If no one has a better idea, I say it's worth a shout. Tha' treasure can't stay 'ere forever, can it?" Grandad follows Max with, "I say we should 'ave a meeting with him. Suss this dodgy Allan out."

"Tim, what do you think?" Asks max. "It can't stay here for long Max, that I think we can all agree on. But we have no clue what it's all worth. There are so many factors to pencil in guys. This dodgy Allan could offer us x amount of money, but how do we know if it's a fair price?"

"I'm with Dylan" says Alice. "It's too risky!"

"Well, that's you two." Sam is now looking around the room, trying to gather support for his plan. Max slouches back in his chair, "Give the guy a call I say."

"I'm with Max on tha'." Replies Grandad. "I like him," utters Daisy "But Tim, what do you think?"

"Perhaps we just reach out, there's no harm in that. We have to start somewhere."

"Yeah, like a proper valuation, so we know what we have and how much it's all worth." Dylan says sarcastically, as he re-enters.

"Well, you're outnumbered Dylan!" Sam announces, and I say, "Unless you have a better plan, then we call him and arrange a meeting."

"He's not coming 'ere, not whilst the treasure's 'ere. Tha's the only thing I've got to add." Says Max. "Can't have people snooping around 'ere."

"Why! What else are you hiding you pirate?" Sam asks. "No, we'll meet him up at the point." Continues Sam.

"Well, that's not going to look at all dodgy then." Comments Dylan.

"That's how he operates, he likes the carpark meetings."

"That's your kinda meeting place ain't it Grandad." Max says laughing.

"Who's going? Cus I bloody ain't, that's for sure!" Says Dylan.

"Nor me!" Says Max still laughing. "I'm not into carpark meetings, take Grandad."

"I'll go, I haven't seen Allan for ages." Daisy exclaims.

"Tim, I want you to come with us both, you'll be better at this stuff than us. I'll just act as the middle man."

"Sure, I was gunna come anyway. Not that I don't trust you or anything, but I feel responsible for this lot." I say, whilst glancing down at the treasure sprawled over the table. Sam gives me an appreciative nod. "So, what's happening with all this in the meantime? We can't stash this sort of stuff in our pants drawer," says Sam. Dylan laughs, "You obviously stash your valuables in your pants drawer then Sam. That's good to know mate." Max starts to walk over to a wall-mounted cupboard. He opens it, revealing a large, beaten-up, rusty safe, "Will this do?" he asks. "Bloody hell Max, how old's that thing?"

"As old as ee is," replies Grandad sniggering.

We carefully wrap the treasure and transfer it into the safe. Max shuts the door, the sound of rusty metal on metal grinds as it locks shut.

"You coming home Grandad?" I ask.

"Not bloody likely. We're staying 'ere, right Max? Guarding tha' treasure we be until its shifted."

That didn't surprise me, as Grandad's already opening another bottle of rum.

*

Sam arranges with Allan to meet the following evening. In the darkness of night, we patiently sit in the carpark at the point, waiting. I'm sat looking out beyond the bay, staring at the distant lights, in a trance. High hopes are certainly something I don't have, but we have to start somewhere. An old, scrappy looking van pulls up alongside us. A tall slim man, wearing jeans and an oversized hoody, jumps out and walks towards us. "Wasson yew legend!" Was the way Allan greet's Sam as we got out of the car. "How's tha' sound system I got yew? Got ee a bargain therr fella, dint I?"

"I think its bloody brilliant Allan." responds Daisy.

"Glad to hear it sweetheart! So, wha's this all about then? Bring me up to speed you lot, I ain't got long."

"Let's walk down to the wall, and we can talk" I say.

Allan wraps his arm around Sam, pulling him in tight as we walk. Together they reminisce and banter back and forth. I interrupt their bromance with, "We've inherited some very old gems and what we believe are very precious stones."

Allan's tone is full of excitement as he asks, "Wha', an old relative left them to yew yeah? Say no more mate, I understand, been in this game long enough. How much are yew after for it then?"

"Well, that's difficult to say really, we have quite a bit."

"Wha', like a big bit?"

"We have a good selection Allan and if it's all real, which we believe it is, then we're guessing it's going to be worth a lot of money."

"I see, so wha' we talking? Hundreds or thousands?"

"Thousands."

"Well, I'm happy to nip round and 'ave a look for yew. And sure, if it's wha' yew say tis, then I'm interested. It's yer lucky day, I've got a few thousand golden nuggets knocking about."

Daisy looks excited with the prospect of having a buyer, whilst Sam's chuffed with himself - thinking he's lined up the deal of the century. "Cool, so I'll tell you what Allan, we'll get it checked so as not to mess you around. If it turns out it's legit, then we'll get Sam to drop you a message."

"Tha's a plan then! Yew give I a message ledg. Guys I'm dashing, got to whizz over to see a chap about a load of chickens ee needs to get shot of. Always on the move me. Later's then, keep I in the loop youngen, yeah? Oh and Shag if you see tha' Max the pirate tell him he stills owes me a ton for tha' rum he had last week."

We watch Allan speed up the road. I look over to Sam and say, "What a waste of time Sam! *Thousands*, what we have guys is going to be worth hundreds of thousands, if not more! The local whealer and dealer isn't our man. What we need is someone who's in that game. You'll have to message him Sam and say it turned out to be fake after all and we're sorry for wasting his time. Hopefully, that will be the end of it. Now let's head back and let the others know that Allan isn't our guy."

"Yeah alright," Sam says in a disappointed tone, "Dylan's gunna flip his lid though, ain't he? He's not gunna let me live this one down."

The journey back to the boatyard is a quite one as Sam and Daisy process the extent of what we'd gotten ourselves into. Selling the treasure is something we'd not fully considered. The office is dimly lit as we walk in, and the others are sat waiting for us to return. Max is sat eating a sandwich and traces of bread crumbs lay scattered in his beard; quite normal for Max.

"How do ee get on then?" he asks whilst chewing aggressively. I get a glimpse of what looks like tuna and cucumber and internally gag a little bit.

"Let's just say Allan's not our guy." I reply.

Sam with a cheeky grin on his face announces "Allan said you still own him money for that rum you had from him, Small world ay max."

"Well, the stoner's come up with another plan!"

"What is it?" I ask. Grandad, pouring more rum, shouts out, "Tis Mr Martin!"

"Mr Martin?" I query. "What about him?"

"Ee's the one that's gunna help sell all this beautiful stuff."

Mr Martin owns an antique and jewellery shop. Rumour has it he once was a big player in London. As I process this idea, everyone seems to agree that Mr Martin was the answer.

Chapter 16

The negotiation

The following morning, we all meet back at the boatyard. Unsurprisingly, both Grandad and Max look terrible.

"Another late night for you two then? This is becoming quite the routine." Daisy giggles.

I announce to the group, "I've spoken to Mr Martin and he's happy to see me this afternoon."

Max grunts, and Grandad just nods. Dylan's brought a large satchel-style bag and his laptop. We spend several hours itemizing all the treasure. Gold and silver coins, diamonds, rubies, sapphires, emeralds, pearls, opals, silver chains, small gold bars, and golden pendants. Max prepares bubble wrap and soft cloth bags which we use to carefully wrap a selection of treasure to show Mr Martin.

*

As we walk through the picturesque streets of our

small-town towards Mr Martin's, I'm aware that we are carrying a very valuable load. Grandad takes on the role of protector, his chest somewhat puffed out and a certain swagger is present in his walk.

Nestled in a quiet part of town, a sign bearing the name 'Martin's Antiques' swings gently in the coastal breeze. As we step through the creaking door, an old brass bell announces our arrival. The first thing that hits me is the scent of aged wood, a hint of polish, and the mustiness of well-preserved history. It's the aroma of stories untold, each piece in the shop holding within it the whispers of its bygone era. The lighting, filters through antique lampshades, casting a warm, muted glow over the array of eclectic items that lined the shelves. The shop's a labyrinth of wonders with dusty trinkets, tarnished silverware, and ornate jewellery displayed in glass cases. Beethoven's 7th Symphony - 2nd movement is playing in the background, adding to the ambience.

Mr Martin stands behind a polished wooden counter. Both Grandad and I know him, not well, but well enough to be welcomed as friends. His long grey hair frames his face. Dressed in a well-worn waistcoat and a crinkled shirt, he exudes an air of both authority and approachability. Floorboards creak beneath our feet as we approach the counter.

"Hello, both. I've been expecting you, after your phone call this morning. I'm intrigued." His London accent commands a certain amount of respect.

"We're hoping you may be able to help us; can we borrow some of your time?"

"Borrow, son?" he replies. "Do you intend on giving it back?"

"We've something we want you to look at."

"How very interesting. Be a delight and switch the sign on the door and flick the handle to lock it young man." Mr Martin leads the way into a back room cloaked by a faded red thick curtain. Inside, interesting pieces not yet unveiled to the public lay in wait. Mr Martin pulls out a chair for Grandad, a beautiful dark wooden table is placed to the side of the room. "Well then, what is it you would like me to look at?"

I place the leather satchel on the table "Before we show you what's in this bag, could I please ask one thing of you?"

"Go forward," is his reply.

"What we're about to show you must remain a complete secret. Can you do this for us?"

Mr Martin pauses for a moment then continues. "Son, I hold so many secrets I'm surprised I'm not working for the government," he laughs. What a random comment, I suddenly feel a little concerned. Grandad opens the satchel and reveals its contents by carefully unwrapping our findings. Gold coins spin around, settling in their place, while gems and jewels sparkle in the dim backlit room. Mr Martin leans in for a better look. "Well, this is a surprise," eyes wide he stares at our collection of treasure, and gently strokes his beard. He rises from his seat and walks over to a set of drawers where he pulls out a magnifying glass, a small jar of clear liquid, and an eye glass. He returns to the table and reaches into the pile of dazzling fortune. He picks up a large diamond, turns on a sharp bright light that's clamped to the edge of the table, and with his eye glass starts to twist and turn the precious stone.

The light bounces off the stone like beams of beauty - magical, almost spiritual. I look up to see Grandad's face full of anticipation and excitement. The atmosphere in the room becomes thick and tense while we wait in silence. Mr Martin places the diamond into the palm of his hand and bounces it up and down, naturally weighing it. He places it to the side without comment and reaches in again, picking up a gold coin. This time, he switches to his large magnifying glass, twisting the coin around and around, moving the magnifying glass in and out. His hands go back in, gently pushing the treasure around, separating it with a tender touch. A small ruby, rich blood-red, catches his attention. Both Grandad and I sit patiently waiting. Mr Martin continues, dance-like with his motions, this time picking up a pearl with a pure black smooth, lustrous surface. My eyes fixate on the pearl's natural form as Mr Martin's hands caress its shape.

He sits back into his chair, and as if in some form of unison, both Grandad and I do exactly the same. He looks at us one by one and moves back towards the table. Again, as if he has captivated us, we synchronize and follow his actions. he rests both elbows on the table and joins his fingers together in a pyramid shape, silent. My hands have become sweaty with anticipation, and Grandad has started to shuffle and fidget in his chair.

"I've decided not to ask where this has come from," Mr Martin says. "What I can tell just by looking at the coins, is that it's Spanish and dates back to the 1700s or there about. But without further inspection, this looks like a collection of real gems and stones." Both Grandad and I turn to each other and smile.

"This is something very special indeed. I haven't seen anything quite like this before, nor shall I again, not in my lifetime. If each item is real and authentic, then you have a very large issue on your hands." Grandad looks at me, somewhat puzzled by his comment. Mr Martin moves his head in slow motion towards me and says. "The only question I'm asking today is what do you intend to do with this treasure?"

"We're looking for confirmation tha' tis all real and authentic," Grandad says.

"If that's the case, I must advise that to be one hundred percent sure, each item will need a much closer inspection, and I'm sure a second opinion will be required. This will take time, as you do have quite a bit here."

"Tha's not all of it," Grandad announces with a slightly embarrassed tone.

"There's more?" Mr Martin asks.

"Um, quite a bit more."

"So again, gentlemen, it brings us back to the only question around this table today. What do you wish to do with it, why have you bought it to me?"

Grandad, nervously responds, "We wish to sell it, sell it all."

"Oh, there we are then," Mr Martin replies. "And there lies your problem."

"Problem?" I ask.

"Yes, young man, problem. If what you have presented to me today turns out to be real, and if as you've stated, there is more, then this could be worth rather a lot of money."

"How much is rather a lot?" asks Grandad.

"There's no fixed price I can give you today sir," Mr Martin replies. "There's many factors to bring into this conversation. The moment you said you wish to sell is the moment you assume there will be a buyer. If you're able to find a buyer, only then would you know the valuation."

"Is that something you could help us with?" I ask. Mr Martin is clearly an expert negotiator, and at that very moment, this became apparent. A sudden shift of character appears as if an actor had just walked onto the stage. His posture and body language undergo a subtle transformation - a calculated stillness that exudes confidence. His tone changes, suddenly increasing in measured authority. Each word chosen with precision, delivered in a calm, confident and composed manner almost like he's reading a script. I instinctively become nervous, perhaps we've bitten off more than we could chew.

"You are asking a lot of me, my dear friends."

"We're asking nothing of you yet, Mr Martin. We've just sought your knowledge, and for that, we are grateful. We wish to sell everything in one go," I say. "It's clear we'll need a buyer, someone prepared to ask no questions and give us a fair price. We can't do this on our own, you may or may not be able to help us but we need someone we can trust and who will be discreet. This person may or may not be you. I look over towards Grandad for backup. Unfortunately, Grandad looks pale and vacant, nothing to do with his age, but alcohol abuse and a lack of sleep has rendered him useless.

Mr Martin, quiet, but is calculated in his response. The question on my mind is, does he have the connections, or is he bluffing? He certainly has an air about him - a big established dealer from London. He looks the part, talks the talk, and certainly knows his stuff but is he just a blagger?

Mr Martin makes his move. A controlled inhalation of air fills his lungs, and with a piercing look straight in my direction, he says, "I know a woman." I glance over at Grandad as this could be our breakthrough moment. Mr Martin continues "This woman has the wealth, she will ask no questions and will give you a fair price, but be warned, she will expect you to abide by her rules and will expect you to be discreet and gentlemanly in all your actions. You'll never meet this woman, and you will ask no questions. I am happy to act as your middleman, connecting you both as you will, but I also have some rules that you must adhere to. I need to know how many people on your side are involved."

"Seven," I respond.

"Are they trustworthy? Think about that question before you answer young man."

"Yes."

"Are they all local?"

Again, "Yes" is my answer.

Mr Martin sits back in his chair. "Okay, you're now going to have to trust me and allow me to hold a small collection of what you have bought in today, I will need to complete an in-depth inspection. The steps of contacting our buyer will not happen until I'm completely one hundred percent, sure that all of this is real. This woman does not take lightly to anyone wasting her time. Is this something you can agree with?"

"Yes," I say.

"Good, then we have a deal." Mr Martin reaches out his hand with confidence to shake mine. His handshake's strong and firm, an alpha male hand shake. I allow him this moment and offer nothing to compete. "Give me one week and I'll call you." He takes a selection of the treasure, then gently pulls back the thick red curtain that separates the back room from the shop.

He walks us to the door, unlocks it, the bell chime confirming our exit. We walk down towards the beach and stop to realign ourselves. Grandad, looking somewhat dazed and confused, still suffering from his hangover, says, "Yew handled tha' well son, good on yew. I thought it best to let yew take the lead."

"Nothing to do with that second bottle of rum then, Grandad?". We head back to the boatyard where the rest of the group are waiting.

When we return, Dylan and Alice are hunched over the laptop researching. Max is sat fixing some netting, a cigarette carefully positioned in his mouth. Sam and Daisy are slouched back in their chairs, drinking tea.

"How did yew get on?" Max is the first to ask. Grandad gathers momentum and starts to explain the experience. He can tell a great story, and although he is jaded by his hangover, he certainly has a good memory as he rattles off the chain of events accurately. Dylan, listening intently, asks, "How do you feel about Mr Martin? Do you think he's trustworthy?"

"As trustworthy as it gets at this stage. At least he seems to know what he's on about, not like our friend dodgy Allan." I respond. "We need to sell all this treasure as soon as possible, and this could be our only option. No doubt he will work in a cut for himself." Dylan's question left me wondering about Mr Martin, is he trustworthy? I guess time will tell and trust is built through time.

Grandad gives a gentle knowing nod, as he looks at Dylan. "Ee's given us no reason why we shouldn't trust him yet Dylan." Grandad slouches back into his usual seat, "I don't think we've any other options, so yes, let's give him the benefit of the doubt."

"He's definitely a strong character, at times slightly intimidating, great with words, talks a good talk, well-educated and knows his stuff. Not sure about his waistcoat though." I say. "He knows how to get what ee wants, tha's for sure," says Grandad. "An interesting man but I agree Son, waistcoats nowadays really?"

"The big concern now is, he knows what we have and that we're desperate to sell. For sure he's going to use this to his advantage," says Dylan.

"There's no doubting that, I could see his mind working overtime, thinking through his options. A master in manipulation. He definitely made me nervous."

"Did he give you any information on the value? Alice and I have been researching, and undoubtedly, if our treasure's real and authentic, then we could be sitting on hundreds of thousands of pounds, if not much more."

I notice Max and Grandad walking off, talking quietly together. Alice notices this too and asks, "What are you both chatting about?"

Grandad glances back, "Last night we were talkin' about security and 'ow best to protect our treasure. We think Max and I should stay for the rest o' the week, keep guard. Especially now Mr Martin knows about the treasure, I reckon we should be extra careful."

Sam chirps up, "Thought that was the plan anyway? But not being rude, what are you old buggers going to do if a gang of robbers turn up?"

Max walks towards his desk, reaches down and grabs what can only be described as a nasty-looking homemade bat, large nails and bolts added to make it appear more terrifying. Max starts swinging his bat around. "What the fuck is that?" Sam asks. Max responds with, "Meet Dug the bat lad."

"If it makes you feel better, then stay. Just go steady on the rum; otherwise, even Dug the bat won't save you. I guess you two together along with that thing is better than nothing."

"One week to wait, then we could all be very wealthy people and I could buy all the mini eggs I want!" Daisy smirks whilst rubbing her hands together. Alice looks over at me with a certain look on her face, expecting backup for what she's about to say next.

"I think we all need to remember why we got involved in the first place. This was always about our community, not about our own personal wealth and gain," Alice states.

Daisy looks confused and responds, "What do you actually mean Alice, with this community thing? I can still buy some mini eggs though, right?"

Alice looks at me, my time to join the conversation, "Alice is right, this was never our treasure. It was always meant to be the communities."

"Agreed," says Dylan. "If we sell the treasure we all have to decide on where the money is going."

Everyone starts looking at each other, waiting for someone to take control of the conversation.

Dylan continues, "I suggest we each take a cut, a personal amount, then donate the rest back into our community to help. Do some good. After all, our community bloody needs it and yes, you can still buy your eggs Daisy."

She follows, "Can we keep something as well though? Something from the stash, a souvenir, you know, a keepsake?" Everyone agrees we should all choose an item to keep. I know what I'm going to choose as my keepsake: a black pearl and I know exactly what I'm doing with it.

Chapter 17

The meeting

My phone begins to ring, displaying Mr Martins number. I hesitate, clearing my mind, preparing for the conversation to follow.

"Hello Mr Martin!"

"Tim, can you pop in to see me regarding the items of jewellery you're interested in please?"

"Yes, that's absolutely fine."

"This afternoon, 2pm?" He asks.

"I'll see you then." I hang up and quickly message Dylan.

Tim: *This afternoon 2pm, Mr Martin wants us to pop into the shop.*

Dylan: *Cool, I'll meet you at Sam's in one hour.*

I follow up with a message to the group chat:

Tim: *I'm meeting Mr Martin at the shop this afternoon to look at some jewellery.*

Max: *Roger that.*

Grandad: *About bloody time.*

When I arrive at Sam's, he's bouncing around as usual, his normal over excited self. Dylan's face says it all, confirming his frustration with Sam, "Calm this one down will you Tim? he's driving me bloody mad." Sam pulls up a chair and with a more serious tone to his voice, and says. "Right you two, this is the plan." Dylan shuts his eyes while simultaneously shaking his head. "You get the best price you can, yeah?"

"Is that it?" Dylan responds. "The biggest moment of our lives and the best you can come up with is that? Sam, you're such a dick!"

"Remember, just be cool lads." Sam adds.

"Right, got that Sam, thanks mate! So glad you're here with your flipping master plan and top advice." Sam rushes off into the kitchen, taking his excitable energy with him. "He's been doing my head in today Tim."

"He's just excited, you know what he's like."

"What is the master plan though?" I ask. "I guess Mr Martin's going to tell us if our treasure's real or not and if the buyer's interested or not. If it's a go, go situation I reckon it's gunna be a delicate balancing act between being keen to sell, but not so keen he takes the piss out of us."

"Who would have thought we'd be negotiating serious money for old treasure?" says Dylan.

"No one I'd rather have by my side dude, you've

got to be more use than Grandad!" We smile and shake hands. "Good luck mate," Dylan says "We just may need it."

*

We head off in the direction of Mr Martin's shop, walking mostly in silence and lost in our own thoughts. The sun's shining and the warmth fills me with hope. I'm extremely nervous though, Mr Martin's holding all the cards, I'm sure he'll love the power and strength that it gives him.

As we enter the shop, Mr Martin appears from behind the thick red curtain. "Good afternoon, no Grandad today?"

"No, not today. But let me introduce you to Dylan, he also has a vested interest in this situation."

"Nice to meet you Dylan," Mr Martin responds, holding out his hand for a formal handshake. "Now, gentlemen, head out to the back and I'll flip the sign and lock the door."

The smell of the shop, captured from my last visit, drifts back with familiarity. "Sit, sit." Mr Martin pulls out the chairs around the table, but he remains standing, dominating the room. It's clear he's relishing his role as the orchestrator.

"You'll be interested to know that I've spent some time with our buyer, and I bring news." He pulls out a chair for himself and now joins us at the table.

"She's extremely interested." I'm aware that he could be playing the game on both sides so brace myself for what's coming. "The samples you have in your possession have all passed the required tests, confirming every item is real and authentic." Dylan looks at me, although trying to remain cool, I can see the excitement on his face.

"That's great news," says Dylan. "So, what's next?" I ask. Mr Martin revives, "What you have in your possession includes Spanish treasure dating back to the 1600s. The circular markings here," He says, whilst pointing to one of the coins, "Tells me that they are rare and of significant value. Our buyer has expressed an interest in purchasing all that you have." He returns to his feet. Back in command, he paces the room with confidence and continues, "However, the rest of the treasure will also need to be inspected and tested to confirm its authenticity."

"We understand," I look at Dylan, who gives a gentle nod of agreement. Mr Martin, now standing with his back to us, replies, "A specialist team will join me for the inspection and valuation."

I'm feeling slightly tense as this situation has now become very real. Mr Martin carries on, "It's been demanded that you must itemize every single piece in your possession and on the day of transaction Tim, only you can be present." The room suddenly feels claustrophobic, almost suffocating.

Slowly wandering and pacing the room, he stops, turning to face us both. "If it materialises that all items are true, original, and authentic, you will be given an offer there and then, there'll be no opportunity to negotiate; the price will be the price. You must also be advised that if you decide to decline the offer the buyer will expect to be compensated for the inspection and valuation process, and their time. This will be at a cost to you of fifty thousand pounds."

Dylan shuffles forward in his seat nervously, his frown signalling his concern. "Fifty thousand pounds?"

"Yes, fifty thousand pounds Dylan. In cash or the equivalent in treasure, it will be your choice."

I can see in Dylan's eyes that this is not sitting comfortably. Mr Martin returns to the table; his demeanour softens but is no less formidable. "At this point, I feel it's worth mentioning to you both that you are in receipt of something you probably shouldn't be and you need to move it on quickly. This will be a very large transaction and will carry a no-questions-asked policy. The sort of people that ask no questions don't mess around, if you know what I mean. There are rules, and you need to know that the rules will not be broken."

Dylan asks, "If we agree, how soon can this happen?"

"Within two days." He replies.

"Can we take a moment please?"

"Yes, I'll pop out and leave you two to discuss your options. I have to pick up something from the post office, now seems a good time." Mr Martin leaves the shop, with the sound of the door closing behind him. I look at Dylan, "What the actual fuck have we got ourselves into? This is heavy shit Dyl."

Dylan calmly responds, "Dude this is good news! Our treasure is real, and we have a buyer. We have a lot of treasure Tim, and as Mr Martin's just pointed out, it doesn't really belong to us. So yeah, we need to get rid of it pretty quickly. This, seems like our only option man, and Mr Martin's the real deal, not like Sam's mate Allan."

"I understand, but are we out of our depth with this whole situation? Dylan, could this be a setup? What if this is a plan to steal the treasure?"

"Dude, you're overthinking this shit, stay cool man."

Dylan grabs hold of my arm and looks at me reassuringly. "It could be a setup dude, but it also could be legit. Right now, we need to decide if we agree, or do we walk away? If we walk away, we have no other options and we're stuck with shit loads of treasure in Max's rusty safe, guarded by two old boys and a home-made bat called Dug. It's clearly worth a lot of money, we're talking a lot of bloody money dude. This could be our chance to cash in, and cash in big time. What's there to think about? Let's commit and take our chance."

"Do you trust Mr Martin?" I ask Dylan.

Dylan without hesitation, "No of course not, I don't trust anyone really, other than you. Sure, he's a bit dodgy, dresses and smells like a seventy's porn star, but one way or another he stands to gain from this, and so do we. So, perhaps we have to trust him."

The sound of the bell rings as Mr Martin returns.

The thick red curtain parts and he joins us back at the table. "Have you talked it through?" he asks.

"We have and we've agreed to go ahead. Can we trust you?"

"*Trust*, before you decide whether you trust me or not, there's one more matter you need to consider; my commission." Mr Martin looks directly into my eyes, with a locked stare. "I will require one hundred thousand pounds to activate this deal and to bring the parties together, do you accept?"

Without thinking I stand, shake his hand. "Agreed," I say. "Two days, you said?"

"Yes, two days."

"Ok, I'll be here, on my own, at 9am this Friday and I'll have all the treasure with me." We shake hands again, but this time I squeeze his just a little bit firmer to show that I'm not intimidated.

I manage to leave the shop calmly with my head held high, but as soon as I get around the corner, the breath that I had been holding in leaves my body through a massive sigh. I head to a nearby wall just to sit, my legs are shaking, I feel sick and dizzy. "Bloody hell, what have we just agreed to?"

"*We*, never agreed to anything Tim. *You*, shook the man's hand at one hundred thousand pounds no questions asked. That's certainly a lot of money for just setting up a deal between two parties!" As Dylan's speaking, I'm just staring at him whilst trying to compose myself, "You okay, dude? You look a little pale." Dylan chuckles, patting me on the back, "You fucking legend mate, I knew you would come through. That's it then Tim, that's the deal. Let's head back to tell the others. You okay to walk, Timmy?"

"Don't take the piss, but you're gunna have to help me off this flippin' wall dude." Dylan reaches out, "Come on you." He grabs me hold and pulls me off the wall. With legs still wobbling, we slowly head back to the boatyard to share the developments, going over the afternoons events as we walk.

*

As we enter the office back at the boatyard, Grandad's the first out of his seat. "Ow did it go then, you two buggers?"

Dylan answers, "This here is one cool dude."

"Well, come on, wha' was said?" asks Max. "Yeah, come on lads, tell us then. Have we made a deal?" Sam asks eagerly.

"There is a deal to be done and it's happening this Friday."

Sam sinks back into his chair, "Shit, that's quick?"

Seeing me still overwhelmed, Dylan takes control. "This is a serious situation we've got ourselves into and you'll need to be aware of a couple of things."

"Go on lad," Max says, whilst signalling Grandad to fetch the rum.

Dylan looks at Max, "Well, once they've checked all the treasure is original and authentic, and they're happy, they'll offer a price there and then. But if we refuse the offer, we have to pay them fifty thousand pounds in cash or in treasure as a form of compensation."

"Compensation? Fifty thousand pounds? Fuck tha'!" Says Max. "For wha'?"

"For their time, Max."

"I'm not paying they'm fuck all."

"What happens if we refuse to pay the fifty grand?" Daisy chirps in.

"We don't. Mr Martin's made it very clear that we don't refuse, I don't think these are the sort of people you refuse."

"Okay, got it." Replies Daisy.

"I have to be at the shop for 9am on Friday. Alone."

"Alone?" Alice asks.

"Yes, just me."

"Anyone else think this is bloody dodgy?" asks Sam.

Alice looks concerned. "Are you sure you're okay with this Tim?"

Dylan jumps in. "Listen guys, we've started this now, and I don't think we could get out of it even if we wanted to."

"He's right," agrees Grandad. "Wha' other options do we 'ave?"

Alice, now pacing the room asks "but how do we know this situation is safe?"

"We don't Alice, we just have to see it through now. We just have to trust Mr Martin."

"Is therr a back entrance to Mr Martins?" Asks Grandad.

"Not sure," Sam quickly checks Google Earth and confirms there is no back entrance to the shop. "If Tim's going in there alone, we need to be sure he'll be safe."

"And how are we going to do that Sam?" Daisy asks, with a desperate tone to her voice.

"Dylan, Sam, are you happy to drop Tim off and wait in the car just up the road? That way, you can monitor any comings and goings." asks Alice.

"No problem, we've got you bro."

"Max and I will go to the Lace and Lime." says Grandad. "We can sit therr all day if needed, Mary will jus' top us up with tea and cake. We can see Mr Martin's from therr so we'll be on hand if therr's any issues"

Looking at Daisy, Alice asks "What about us?"

"Let's treat ourselves to a new tattoo. We can hang out with Roxy. If any problems arise, we'll just be up the road too."

"You can get my name tattooed as a token of our love." Suggests Sam. "As if!" Daisy laughs.

Chapter 18

Behind the red curtain

I check the time, and it's bang on 9am as I grab the bag of treasure from the boot. Nervously, I glance back towards Sam and Dylan one last time as I walk towards Mr Martin's shop entrance. I notice that there's no lights on, my heart begins to pound, not knowing what to expect. My hands are shaking where I'm gripping the handle of the bag so tightly. I look over to see Max and Grandad sitting in the window of Lace and Lime, true to their word, already eating cake and drinking tea. I take a deep breath to steady my anxiety as I knock on the door. From behind the red curtain, I can see Mr Martin appear, he's smartly dressed as always, but his posture is different and he looks nervous.

Mr Martin unlocks the door and greets me with his usual firm handshake. "Good morning Tim, they're waiting inside." He ushers me towards the red curtain, he stops and looks directly into my eyes, asking, "Are you ready for this young man?"

His right hand reaches out and he firmly places it on my shoulder.

"Remember the rules. Don't break any of the rules Tim, not today."

I respond with a reassuring but nervous tone "I don't intend to." Mr Martin pulls back the red curtain and I quickly scan the room. Sitting around the table are three men and a woman, all smartly dressed, professional looking. One of the men has a distinctive scar across his right cheek. My attention is drawn to the back of the room where a man stands alone. This man's different. At first glance, he's in his late forties, or thereabouts. He's a large, very muscular and aggressive looking man, standing tall and proud. He's got a shaven head with neck and hand tattoos; his hands are massive. He's dressed in a black bomber-style jacket, clearly the security man and certainly someone not to be messed with. Perhaps that's why Mr Martin seems on edge. Shit, he's a big dude with big hands. Beside him are two very large black holdall bags.

"Tim, can you please place the bag on the table and take a seat. The process of checking the treasure will now begin." Not one person spoke, which makes me feel very uneasy. Each person around the table seems to know exactly the role they have to play. One has a magnifying glass along with a head torch. The woman has several jars of solutions, a dark green cleaning cloth and a weighing machine. The man at the rear of the table, 'Scar Face,' has an interesting leather-bound old-looking book with pictures, likely a reference book of some sort. I can see charts and tables on his iPad in the reflection of a glass cupboard. Another person takes photos of each item, he also has bags, boxes and bubble wrap at the ready. It looks like there is definitely a system in place.

I sit fascinated and fixated as each person plays their role, still without speaking. They show no emotion or excitement. Every sound magnified by the quiet. The soft stirring of the solution in the glass container creates a gentle clinking of metal against glass cutting through the silence. The camera's shutter snaps closed, sharp and precise. The thin paper of the old book, fragile as it's handled.

It seems that they communicate solely by looking at each other; nods, and hand gestures, but no talking. The system plays out for several hours, back and forth, with each person looking intently, cleaning, measuring, weighing, recording, and photographing. One by one, each item's checked, and bagged or boxed. It's 11:10 am when suddenly a knock on the shop door interrupts the silence. Nobody at the table flinches or breaks their concentration but Mr Martin stands up immediately to walk out into the shop.

"No!" The big dude at the back of the room commands in a deep voice. "Are you expecting anyone?"

"No." Mr Martin replies, sheepishly.

"Well, sit back down please sir." Mr Martin sits back down immediately, and he glances over with an expression of surprise. It's somewhat entertaining to see Mr Martin put in his place.

I'm left with my thoughts. I avoid eye contact with

Big Hands but the bags have captured my attention. What if they're stuffed with cash? What if there's no cash but guns? Am I about to be robbed? My imagination is running wild as I work through different scenarios, entertaining myself whilst waiting.

The process continues, I look again and it's now 1 p.m. Thankfully, the last of the items are being checked. Four hours have passed without anyone moving, not even Big Hands. He's stayed solid in the same position, watching and guarding. As the last item goes through its checks, Scarface stands up and asks, "Can we please talk, Mr Martin?"

The man walks out to a back area beyond a door marked private, Mr Martin follows. They're gone for some time before Mr Martin returns to the room.

"Can I have a word Tim?" He asks, "Follow me, please."

I stand up somewhat awkwardly, as my whole body has been in one position for so long. I can't help but feel scared and anxious for what waits beyond the door. My heart rate quickens as I follow.

Behind the door is a thin long corridor leading to what looks like a toilet. The space is dimly lit and cold, boxes, cardboard, and some old paint pots are pushed up against the wall. The man's now talking on his phone, pacing up and down. The conversation goes on for a while, although I can't really hear what's being said. As the call ends, he walks back towards me, "I can confirm that all of the treasure you've brought in today is authentic, original, and true."

Stunned in the moment, I think to myself, what next? Too scared to ask, I stand there frozen, just silently waiting.

The man continues, "A price has been agreed." I look over at Mr Martin, who simply says, "Good, that's good news." He quickly turns to me with an encouraging smile. Before I have a chance to say anything, the man continues, "One million, seven hundred thousand pounds is the offer. Do you accept?" Mr Martin looks at me again, this time with intent in his eyes, prompting me to say yes. My mouth's dry, and that number is way more than I was expecting. As calmly as I can, I respond, "Yes, yes, I do."

Without expression, the man starts to message someone. I'm shocked and completely overwhelmed. Could it be true? Had I heard that amount, right? The man then says, in a firm direct voice, "There are no comebacks with this arrangement. Do you fully understand?"

"We understand." We say. I can hear lots of movement back in the room, where the treasure is being checked. What's happening now? My mind, fearing the worst. Paranoia's running riot. What if they're leaving with the treasure? What then? The man stands very still, just looking at us both in silence. Why are we waiting? What's happening? Minutes pass. A message alert comes through on the man's phone and he walks straight past us, back into the room. Both Mr Martin and I look at each other apprehensively, we hear the bell of the shop door as it opens and closes. No more sound, just quiet.

"What now?" I ask.

"I'm not really sure," replies Mr Martin. He slowly opens the door and peers around. "They've all gone." I feel an emptiness inside, what if we've been robbed? What if they've taken the treasure and just left? As I walk back into the empty room, there placed on the table are the two large kit-style bags. We both stand just looking at them, terrified to move.

"Well Tim, we're either a little richer than we were this morning, or we've just been completely done over." I'm still not sure if I trust Mr Martin, so comments like this don't help. He could quite easily have set this whole thing up and pocketed all the treasure for himself. My anxiety races to an all-time high.

"You unzip it Tim." I take a moment to compose myself. Leaning in gently I start unzipping. The first thing that hits me is a sweet slightly musty smell, nothing I'd ever smelt before. Right there, is more money than I could ever comprehend - packed in bundles of fifty and twenty-pound notes, the bag's full. Absolutely full.

"I'm checking the door," Mr Martin says scurrying off to check the shop door's locked. In no time, he's back in the room, quickly shutting the red curtain behind him. "Jackpot!" He says. "That seems to be rather a lot of money young man." I look up at him, grinning. "Is this what one million, seven hundred thousand pounds looks like?" I ask. "Open the other one." He demands, with an impatient excitable tone. Sure enough, the second is also stuffed with money.

"Let's count it."

"Count it? Mr Martin, are you mad? That's a lot of money for us to count, it will take ages!"

"Not if you have one of these," He says, he reaches into a cupboard and pulls out a money-counting machine. The smell of all the cash has now taken over my senses, and I'm almost delirious with the sight of it all.

Messages flood in from a now overly concerned crew as they've watched the people leaving. Quickly I respond with:

Tim: *It's all good guys but I need more time.*

Mr Martin grabs a large bundle of fifty-pound notes, and places them in to the counting machine. The noise is rhythmic and loud as the money speeds through. Hunched over, we both watch with excitement. The machine confirms fifty thousand pounds. Mr Martin continues to repeat the process, bundle after bundle. I stack them in rows of fifty thousand pounds. Soon, we have one million pounds. The whole room now smells of a sweet, inky aroma. The process continues until the entire table is covered.

"One million seven hundred thousand pounds," Mr Martin confirms. "It's all there Tim."

We stand back in amazement, the whole room filled with piles of money. "We did it! Mr Martin I can't thank you enough, this wouldn't have happened without you."

He looks over with a humble expression, something I've not witnessed before. His new posture makes him seem vulnerable, normal. "To be honest with you Tim, this was a gamble and I had my doubts that we'd pull it off. I have done plenty of deals in the past but this one, well it's by far the biggest. This one's kept me up at night."

"How scared were you this morning?" I ask.

"As much as you I think Tim, but between us, we kept our nerve well."

I pull out my phone and message.

Tim: *It's done! Dylan, bring the car to the front of Mr Martin's please, I have rather a heavy load to carry.*

Instantly, a thumbs-up returns.

"Well, Mr Martin, from the bottom of my heart, I truly want to thank you." A handshake seems... well, not enough, so I hug him tight. I reach for two bundles of fifty thousand pounds and hand them to him, "I believe this is yours, you've truly earnt it."

"What are you planning to do with all this money?" he asks.

"It's going back into the community one way or another."

He helps me put all the money back into the bags, which are now ridiculously heavy. Watching me struggle, "I'll get the door," He says. Outside, Dylan and Sam are waiting with the boot open. As I put them into the boot, Mr Martin says, "This has been quite an adventure for this old man." He winks, pats me on the arm, and returns inside, flipping the closed sign behind him.

I sit in the front passenger seat of the car and look over at Dylan. "Can we please drive back to the boatyard now guys? We have one million, six hundred thousand pounds in cash in your boot. Please drive carefully, Dylan." Sam, in shock, sinks back into his seat "shit that's a lot of cash". Dylan looks over and nods, "I'll drive extra bloody carefully today then lads."

Chapter 19

The smell

We're the first to arrive back at the boatyard. Dylan flicks the lights on in the office and places the two large loads carefully on the table. Exhausted, I collapse into a chair.

"Will one of you please open a bag and check I'm not dreaming?"

Sam, nervously pacing the room, mutters, "I can't do it lads, I can't do it. Dyl, it's gotta be you, you do it."

Dylan hesitates, then slowly unzips one. The smell of sweet ink fills the air, a sharp undeniable reminder that this isn't a dream. The reality sinks in, and Dylan finally breaks the silence with a drawn-out, "Fuuuckin' hell." The words hang heavy in the room as he opens the second bag. In disbelief, he stumbles to a chair, his face frozen in a mix of shock and awe.

Sam's voice cuts through the tension as he inches closer, sniffing, eyes wide. "That smell, it's like nothing I've ever smelt before." Dylan shakes off his daze, a grin creeping onto his face. "That's because you've never had this much cash stuffed in your pants drawer before mate."

Just then, Max and Grandad walk in. Max's nose twitches, with a knowing smile. "Tha's cash!" He laughs, rubbing his hands together. Grandad, noticing me slumped in my chair, strides over, concern etched across his face. He bends down, eyes searching mine. "Yew alright son, yer looking a bit in shock?"

Max peers into the bags, "Yew better take a look at this lot Grandad." Grandad pats me on the back, murmuring, "You're alright son." He makes his way to join Max who's standing, transfixed. Grandad wraps an arm around Max's shoulder, steadying himself as he leans in. Both remain silent, locked in place, staring down at the massive amount of cash.

"How much is in 'ere then?" Max finally asks, his voice barely a whisper.

"One million, six hundred thousand pounds." Dylan replies.

I watch as Grandad's face changes, his eyes brightening, his grip on Max tightening. A tear escapes down his weathered cheek. This is the moment he's waited for, after years of struggle and loss. Standing there, he looks triumphant and proud. For the first time, I feel it too; a fierce pride in what we've managed to achieve together.

The door bursts open, and Daisy and Alice bundle into the office. Their voices overlapping as they both ask how it went in their own ways. Daisy pauses, her nose wrinkling. "What's that smell?"

"That's the smell of a bloody fortune love," Sam says with a grin.

Alice crosses the room, and kneels beside me, her hand finds my leg, grounding me. "You alright Beach Boy?" she asks gently.

I let out a long breath, feeling the weight of the day finally sinking in. "It's been a... long, interesting, and slightly stressful day." She smiles, pulling me into a hug. The warmth of her body is exactly what I need. "It's over now," she reassures, her voice soothing.

"How much did we get?" Daisy asks, glancing towards the bags.

"One million, seven hundred thousand pounds, minus one hundred thousand for Mr Martin, as agreed." Dylan replies.

Alice raises her eyebrows, giving me a playful nudge. "Is that all?" she laughs, holding me tighter. "No wonder you're stressed Beach Boy."

"Did you get your tattoo done?" She pulls up her dress, revealing a beautiful silhouette tattoo on the back of her calf, it's still wrapped in cling film, slightly bloody. A man and a woman sitting on a longboard under a starlit sky, the word hope scrolling elegantly along the bottom. "That's beautiful."

Alice helps me up, and we all gather around the table, gazing at the bags filled with cash. Grandad, his arm still tightly around Max, lets out a choked laugh. "Well, we did it yew lot," his voice thick with emotion.

"Who'd 'ave thought we'd be standing 'ere, staring at this much cash?"

Alice reaches down, taking Grandad's hand. Max, his voice wavering, adds, "Yew lot 'ave become family to me, these past few months… it's been a hell of an adventure and I've loved it. Thank yew guys" Daisy leans in, giving Max a daughter-to-father style hug. Silence falls over us as we take in the unbelievable sight, each lost in our own thoughts, processing this life-changing moment.

Sam speaks up, breaking the silence. "Just putting it out there, will this lot even fit in the safe?"

Laughter breaks out, Daisy gives Sam a playful shove. "Let's celebrate!" Alice shouts. Max beams, his voice full of excitement, "Get tha' bloody rum Grandad! And them cigars! Wherr's they cigars?"

"I'll roll a fat one," Dylan adds with a grin, catching Sam's eye, "Chuck me the skins mate."

"Hold on!" Alice shouts, her voice breaking through the rising excitement. She looks straight at the bags. "Before we all lose our way tonight, can I please check, who's staying here to keep an eye on this lot?"

"We all are!" Comes the enthusiastic response in unison. Laughter ripples through and the celebrations begin. Daisy pairs her phone to Max's old, battered Bluetooth speaker, and suddenly, 'Beautiful Day' fills the room. Sam starts bouncing around, as if he's an eight-year-old at his first ever disco, while Dylan belts out the lyrics, arms lifted as if the music itself could carry him away. Alice grabs me and starts spinning us in circles, our laughter blending with the song. Max, already sipping rum, stomps in rhythm, and Daisy links arms with Grandad, both of them laughing with such joy that it brings tears to their eyes. In that moment, we're all weightless, bound together by more than blood or friendship, free at last. The fever of excitement grows as the night promises to be a wild one.

*

I move my head ever so slowly; my neck hurts and it's stiff. I've fallen asleep awkwardly in the chair and Alice is curled up on my lap, her head resting gently on my chest. Opening my eyes feels like prising apart something glued shut, and my mouth is painfully dry. The room is silent now, that eerie quiet of the morning after. An overwhelming sense of last night's revelry sinks in, a cocktail of stale tobacco, inky cash and rum fills the air, souring my stomach and adding to my feeling of nausea.

Squinting, I scan the room. Everyone seems to have crashed in somewhat interesting positions: Max and Grandad are still at the table, arms draped protectively over the bags. Max has Dug strategically positioned to the side of him, whilst Grandad's snoring echoes around the room. Daisy and Sam have somehow slumped into sleep, sitting upright against the door, while Dylan lies curled up in a tight ball under the table, using his arm as a makeshift pillow.

A faint groan escapes Alice as she stirs. "Morning...

Did I tell you yet how much I love you, Beach Boy?" She murmurs.

One by one, everyone wakes up, stretching, yawning, and squinting as the morning low light filters into the office.

"My fucking head," Sam groans, rubbing his temples. Max, in slow motion, raises his head groggily from the position it had found last night. He looks around confused, as if he is searching for something. There it is, a glass half full of rum. He reaches out, picking up the glass and lifts it to his mouth, where he consumes the remains and then gently rests his head back down closing his eyes.

Life starts trickling back into the room.

"Got any food Max?" Sam asks, holding his head as he gets to his feet. Max gestures toward a half-open packet of biscuits on the table. "Knock yerself out lad."

Grandad joins the awakening club and asks, "Where's Dylan?" A grunting sound emerges from under the table as it seems Grandad has unwittingly discovered Dylan's location, kicking him as he stretches out.

With a mouth full of biscuits, Sam stares at the bags. "So, are we deciding today what we're doing with this lot then? Because there's no way I'm sleeping here with you nutters again tonight-not a bloody chance. Just look at the state of you all, you should be ashamed, especially you too old buggers, you should know better and be setting an example."

As Sam munches through Max's stash of biscuits,

Dylan slowly emerges from under the table, crawling backwards. "Morning all. Anyone seen me baccy?"

"Sam's got a point," Daisy says, her voice hushed but steady. "What are we planning to do with all this money then?"

We gather around the table, each of us looking worse for wear. Grandad sits with his head in his hands, Sam with dried biscuit crumbs scattered across his mouth, and the rest of us barely holding ourselves upright. "So, wha's the plan?" Grandad finally asks, "What's everyone thinking?"

"Therr's no thinking going on at the moment," Max mutters, the fatigue deepening his usual gruffness.

We start talking through our options, sharing fragmented ideas and half-formed plans for how to use the money to benefit the community. Conversations go back and forth, often looping back to the same points, many of our suggestions jumbled by lack of sleep. But slowly, clarity starts to form. We agree: each of us will keep one hundred thousand pounds, leaving nine hundred thousand to pour back into the place we all call home.

"I have one request, if I may?" Dylan asks "Can I bung some cash in envelopes and post them through doors? I know it sounds random, but how exciting would it be for people to find envelopes with cash in? A random act of kindness."

"I would like to support local businesses," says Sam. "Can we give some money to all of the businesses around? We could do the same idea and just pop envelopes of cash through the doors of each business, keeping it anonymous, what a laugh we could have."

"Can we also donate some money to the surf school?" Alice asks.

Dylan, rolling a fag, suggests, "What about funding some youth projects? The kids from around here would benefit so much."

I start to jot down all the ideas as the room suddenly explodes with requests.

Lydia appears at the forefront of my mind. "Can we give Lydia some of the money? She's been trying to get her community project up and running for ages. She cares so much about the wellbeing of our community, I can't think of a worthier cause to fund."

"Can we give to local charities?" asks Daisy.

Grandad, now on his second brew, looking more alive, demands attention. Clearing his voice, he brings the focus of the chatter back to him. "I need yew all to agree, this whole situation, giving out money and tha' must stay completely anonymous. We can't afford this lot to be traced back to us. I'm sure wha' we're doing ain't fully legal and I'm far too old to do a stretch, I'm more of an outdoor kinda guy." We all agree and pledge that no one will ever know where the money has come from and it will remain a secret.

Once we've divided up the amounts and decided who gets what, Alice suggests "Let's hold some money back and throw a massive party down at Bottom Beach for all the locals."

Max becomes frustrated with the chatter and noise of the room his hangover is apparent as he stands up stretching and with a grumpy tone say "Listen to yew all planning to solve everyone's problems with yer money. Money don't bring people happiness yew know. If people are miserable buggers then therr miserable buggers. He lights up a rolly clears his voice and contuines "no amount of cash will make them happy. This act of kindness ain't going to change people."

Dylan replies trying to diffuse Max's comment. "It's not about changing people Max it's about giving them something, a boost. You know like that feeling when you find a tenner in your pocket you'd forgot about It feel good yeah, a nice surprise that's all were doing just a little something for people to enjoy.

"You're the one being miserable now Max" Laughs Daisy.

Chapter 20

Random acts of kindness

Over the next few months, our secret mission unfolds. Envelopes and parcels of cash, with the word 'Hope' printed on, are distributed and delivered as agreed. We have so much fun, undercover, often in the darkness of night, changing people's lives one envelope and parcel at a time. Sneaking into businesses, leaving bundles of cash, knowing what a difference we were making filled our hearts with joy and felt so right.

The reaction was beyond anything we could have imagined. Our home came to life with stories and rumours about large sums of money appearing, delivered by angels some said.

Myself and Dylan hitch a plan to leave a box of cash in the boot of Lydia's car. It's a Tuesday evening and the Salty Seagull is alive with the sound of proud voices and melodies from the evening's sea shanties. Lydia's jigging with some locals, lost in the music. The pub is buzzing, the low hum of chatter blending with the rhythm of the different musical instruments.

"How are we doing this, then, Dylan?" I ask, but he doesn't respond.

"Dylan? Dylan!" I say louder. He's completely drawn into the atmosphere, foot tapping along to the energy created by the instruments and singing.

"Sorry, dude. You were saying?"

I lean in and whisper, "If you keep her distracted, I'll nip out the back and take her car keys."

Dylan frowns, "How am I supposed to keep her distracted?"

"Just go over, you fool, stand with her and keep your eye on her. Just don't let her out of your sight."

Dylan's slightly awkward in social situations, he hesitates, shifting uneasily.

"You ready?" I ask.

"Sure. Just stand with her, yeah?" he mutters heading off in her direction.

I watch as he slowly makes his way through the crowd, moving towards Lydia. The warmth of the room pulsing with the music. The moment he reaches her, I slip away, and weave through people toward the staff room. I waste no time in search of Lydia's bag. As soon as I find it, my fingers start searching for her keys. As I sift through her belongings, the door creaks open behind me.

"You all right there, Tim?" I freeze, my heart pounding. It's the owner. "Fine," I say quickly, turning to see her standing in the doorway. "Just getting Lydia's keys for her and we're about to grab a quick break, if that's okay boss?" I wait, watching for any sign of suspicion. She lingers for a moment before nodding in approval and picking up her cardigan from the chair, disappearing back towards the bar. Releasing a slow breath, I make my way outside to the car park.

With a quick glance around, I unlock Lydia's car and place the box carefully in the boot. Then, I drop an envelope onto the seat, our trademark **HOPE** scrawled across it. Inside is a note that reads 'Look in your boot and dream big.'

I quietly shut the car, making sure not to draw attention to myself, and head back inside.

Re-entering the pub, I scan the room. I search for Dylan and Lydia, but they're nowhere to be seen. Where are they? Then, from the corner of my eye, I spot them at the far end of the bar. Dylan looks different, his posture's more relaxed, his face lit up with a big smile.

I smirk. Dylan's having a moment, cute. They're perfect for each other, how had I not seen it before? Moments later, Dylan returns and he's practically glowing.

"You all right, dude?" I ask, raising an eyebrow.

He grins. "She's proper lush man and I've only gone and plucked up the courage to get her flipping number!"

I chuckle. "She's a beautiful soul, that's for sure." Dylan proudly nods in agreement and asks, "Did you find her keys?"

"Yeah, it's done."

At the end of the night, we can't help ourselves; we have to see Lydia's reaction when she gets into her car. Trying not to be obvious, we linger outside, pretending to chat while watching as she unlocks her car. She notices the envelope on the seat straight away, picking it up hesitantly. She glances around, almost nervous, before finally opening it. Still hesitant, she moves towards the boot. Inside, in a simple box, is a life-changing amount of cash. Watching her face as she struggles to comprehend what's just happened to her was amazing. Giving out money to people and knowing what a difference it was making is the best feeling ever.

*

Not long after, Lydia buys some land, and her dream begins to take shape. A community space, a project that will have such a positive impact on so many lives. A place where everyone can come together, connect with each other and feel part of something unique.

Daisy saw to it that local charities benefitted as well. A new bright yellow minibus now belonging to the charity 'Rag Doll' trundled around the area, with excited faces waving from sticky finger-smudge windows, heading off on adventures they'll never forget.

Dylan's youth projects included art classes on the beach, bringing together local artists and inspiring the next generation through the love of creativity. He seems to have one person regularly helping and supporting him though. Lydia also has a strong creative flair and they naturally work in harmony together. They are both in their element and are so good at supporting people whilst bringing the best out of them.

Alice saw that the surf schools' doors continued to open, sharing her passion for the power of the ocean.

*

I find myself watching Alice from a distance and it reminds me of the very first day I saw her. I was sat outside Sam's café, drinking hot chocolate with sweaty hands and wondering if one day I would ever have the confidence to talk to her. She notices me and runs over smiling. She jumps on me with force, nearly knocking me over. "Remember Beach Boy, our journey always included you learning to surf. So, come on, it's time!" Alice grabs my hand hold and drags me to the surf schools' entrance. "Des, get this young man a suit! He's joining in the fun today."

The breeze rolls in, carrying the rhythmic crash of waves against the shoreline. As I zip up in my wetsuit, I stumble towards a group of young people. They all look so, supple, nimble and quick. Already, I feel this was going to be one of those forever embarrassing moments that was going to stay with me for the rest of my life.

Alice, standing confidently, claps her hands together. "Alright, team! Before we hit the water, we need to go through some basics." She calls out, her voice carrying over the sound of the waves. The young new surfers, a mix of eager and nervous faces, nod and watch her closely.

Now in full command, Alice picks up her board and sets it down on the sand. "Okay, first things first - paddle position. Lie flat on your board, chest up, hands by your shoulders. You want smooth, even strokes when you paddle out."

The young surfers enthusiastically drop onto their boards, mimicking Alice's movements with surprising ease. However, I hesitate before lowering myself onto my board, still feeling completely out of my depth.

"Great! Now, when you're ready to pop up, it's all about timing and balance. Watch me first." Alice effortlessly demonstrates, springing up in one smooth motion, her feet landing perfectly in place. "One foot forward, knees slightly bent, arms out for balance."

The group follows her lead, some wobbling but managing to find their footing. As I push up, my arms are slightly shaking and as soon as I try to bring my foot forward, the board slips from beneath me. I flop onto the sand with an *oomph*.

A chuckle ripples through the group. Alice smirks but holds back from laughing. "It's all good, Tim. Just take it slow. Let's break it down, step by step." I sit up, brushing the sand from my hands and try to hide my embarrassment.

Alice wanders over, dropping into a crouch beside me and whispers, "Try this. Start by pushing up onto your knees first, get steady before you bring your foot forward."

I take a deep breath and try again. This time, I manage to get to my knees before wobbling into an awkward crouch.

"Better!" Alice praises. "Now, when we get in the water, the key is to read the waves. You don't just stand up the moment you feel like it. You wait. It's about feeling the ocean beneath you, moving with it, not against it. Look for the signs."

The young surfers nod, taking in her every word. I'm still kneeling on my board, watching the waves roll in, their white foam curling onto the shore. Maybe Alice is right. Maybe this is less about brute force and more about feeling the rhythm of the sea. I practise a few more times, paddle, paddle-up, paddle, paddle-up. Already my legs are burning and my balance, well, it's a bit off to say the least.

One big deep breath in. "Okay, let's do this."

Alice winks. "That's the spirit. Now, let's get wet!"

The group charges towards the waves, boards tucked under their arms. I stand back and hesitate at the shoreline, watching as the others dive forward onto their boards and paddle effortlessly past the breaking waves. I swallow hard, as Alice shoves me in the back and says "In you go!"

I wade in, gripping my board as the first wave

crashes against my legs, nearly knocking me off balance. I throw myself onto my board and start paddling. The motion feeling clumsy, my arms heavy against the resistance of the sea.

Meanwhile, the others are already sitting confidently on their boards, waiting for Alice's next cue. They make it look so simple, balancing easily, as if they've been doing it all their lives. I, however, am still battling to keep my board steady beneath me, my chest and arms burning from the effort.

"Okay, guys, eyes on the horizon!" Alice calls out. "Here comes a good set, get ready!"

With a practiced ease, she pivots her board and begins paddling as the first swell lifts her. In one fluid motion, she pops up, her body instinctively finding balance as she rides the wave towards the shore. The young surfers follow her lead, some wobbling but managing to stay upright, their cheers ringing out as they glide over the water.

I watch, frustration bubbling. How the hell are they doing this so easily?

"Come on, Tim, you've got this!" Alice shouts encouragingly, paddling back towards me. "Just focus on catching the right wave, wait for it, feel it beneath you, and commit."

I grit my teeth and turn my board, copying the others. A wave approaches, and I start paddling furiously, arms flailing as I try to match its speed. The swell lifts me, I push up and try to find my footing and balance, but the board jerks violently beneath me.

Before I can react, I'm tumbling into the water. Salty liquid fills my nose and mouth as I'm dragged under, rolling around as if I was in a washing machine.

I surface, spluttering, my board floating a few feet away. Alice paddles beside me, her eyes twinkling with amusement.

"Not quite," she teases. "But you didn't drown, so that's a win."

"You're overthinking it," Alice says gently. "You don't have to fight the ocean, you have to move with it, become part of it. Try again."

I retrieve my board and paddle back out. The others are now riding waves consistently, growing more confident with each attempt. If they can do it, so can I.

Alice points to an incoming wave. "This one's yours, go for it!"

I start to paddle as hard as I could. The swell picks me up again, and this time, I try to feel the motion. As I push up, it feels steadier than before, I place one foot forward. The board wobbles, but I fight to stay upright. Don't panic, feel the wave, move with it - is my focus.

And then it happens.

For a few glorious seconds, I'm standing. The wave carries me forward, salt spraying in my face, the world tilting in a rush of exhilaration. I'm doing it! I'm actually surfing!

Alice throws her hands in the air. "Yes, Beach Boy! You're surfing!"

Just as I process the moment, my board wobbles, and I topple sideways into the water.

Alice paddles over, beaming. "That was amazing! You actually rode your first wave!"

I run my hands through my dripping hair, breathless, "That was brilliant what a rush."

She nods proudly, "See? Told you. You just had to trust yourself."

I look back at the endless horizon, my body still buzzing from the ride. For the first time, I understand why Alice loves this. The power of the ocean, the thrill of the waves pushing you forward, the pure freedom of it all. What a feeling! climbing back onto my board with newfound confidence I paddle out, I want to go again, I'm hooked!

Chapter 21

I will

I head to Sam's Café to meet the crew as its opening day, after the big refurbishment. The sun hangs high in the sky, flooding the streets with warm light, filling me with a rush of optimism. I notice people everywhere, talking and smiling, their energy infectious. There's a renewed pride in the community, a quiet sense of purpose that seems to flow through everyone, drawing people closer. We're social creatures at heart; this now reminds me why communities are so important. Our act of kindness has helped people to reconnect.

As I approach the Café, I spot Sam standing alone, eyes scanning over the place like he's seeing it for the first time. "Dude, look at this place! You must be so pleased with how it's turned out." Sam faces me, and before I know it, he's pulling me into a hug, tight and grateful.

"It's better than I ever could have imagined."

The Café's had a full make over, but the rustic charm remains; weathered wood and old signs preserved to hold onto its history, the tables packed with people laughing, enjoying the breeze and the sea's salty scent.

"I love it Sam," I say, and I mean it. This Café has always been part of our lives, but now it's like a new chapter waiting to be written.

Daisy is buzzing around the tables outside, serving food and drinks, she looks so happy. Sam leans in close to me, his voice low and serious.

"I'm going to ask her Tim."

"What you on about mate?" Though I have a feeling I know what's coming.

"I'm going to ask Daisy to marry me. She's the one, isn't she?"

I nod, feeling a rush of excitement for him. "Yeah, she's the one Sam. It's about bloody time, too."

Sharing that special moment with him, I catch sight of Alice, Max, and Grandad laughing together in the crowd. Alice's natural beauty has always had me captivated, and for a moment, I imagine one day looking into her eyes and asking her to marry me.

"What are you lovers talking about?" A voice boom's from behind, Dylan's arms wrap around our shoulders, his presence as bold as his look. He's decked out like a '70s rock star; shirt half-open, a large pendant swinging over his bare chest, denim flares grazing his ankles and barefoot of course. Dylan's latest 'grounding' phase, apparently connecting with the earth, he claims it's the way forward for health and wellbeing.

"I'm gunna ask her mate," Sam says, barely containing his nerves.

"Ask her what? You weirdo." Dylan looks at me and raises a brow.

"I'm gunna ask Daisy to marry me!"

"Cute," Dylan smirks, patting him on the back. "About bloody time, you two are made for each other everyone knows that."

He catches my eye, mouthing "stag do" with a wink.

As we approach, I notice Alice shaking her head, a faint smile playing at the corners of her mouth. Grandad glances at Dylan, "What've yew come as lad? This ain't a fancy-dress party, yew know."

Alice, struggling to keep a straight face, announces, "You'll never believe what these two have gone and done." She gestures over to the car park. I turn, and there, parked proudly among the usual cars and vans, sits a slightly battered, classic American Winnebago RV. It's old and battered, but Max and Grandad look positively delighted with it.

"Tha's ours," Grandad says. "She's called Honey." The two of them clink their mugs, grinning.

"We're heading to Scotland next week," Max adds.

Grandad turns to Dylan, his gaze suddenly serious. "Tha' reminds me, hippy boy, I need a word."

Dylan chuckles. "I know what you're gunna ask Grandad and yeah, I'll sort you out."

Another clink of mugs, and laughter fills the air.

"Have you told Mum about this new adventure Grandad?"

"She knows and she ain't so 'appy about it son."

He pauses, then nods toward the shore. "Walk with me son will yew?"

We head down to the water's edge, where the sea stretches out, endless and calm. Grandad stops, eyes fixed on the horizon. "There's something I want to talk to yew about, about your Mum. She's always been therr for us both, done her best, and… I think 'tis time she knows jus' how much we appreciate her."

I glance over, unsure where this is going. "Where's this heading, Grandad?"

He takes a breath, then faces me. "I want to pay off her mortgage, take some weight off her shoulders but, yew know her, she won't jus' take the money. She'll ask a hundred questions, and we can't tell her the truth, can we?"

I nod in agreement, knowing Mum definitely would ask questions. "So, what's your plan?"

"We sell your Dad's boat and tell her tha's where the money came from. She doesn't have a clue how much 'tis worth, and so she won't be suspicious."

My chest tightens. "Dad's boat?"

Grandad nods, his gaze steady. "Yes, your Dad's boat, but only if yew agree. I couldn't let go of her before, too many memories and too much history. But now... it feels right."

The words hit hard, I look away, grappling with the thought of letting go. Grandad rests a hand on my shoulder. "It's the right thing son. The past is the past now. Maybe 'tis time we all moved forward."

I imagine the empty driveway, the memories tied up in that boat, the secret meetings Grandad and I had on her, but he's right; maybe it's time. Mum would be thrilled to see it gone, and Grandad's plan... it makes sense. "Max has a buyer lined up, and it's a good price. We could pay off the mortgage, even send Mum on a holiday - a real break, somewhere far away."

As the waves lap gently at the shore, Grandad's words settle over me, he's got a point. The memories will always stay with me. "I think you're right Grandad. It's time to let go, this will be the new beginning we all need." He smiles, then gives me a gentle shove which is his own way of showing affection. I bend down, pick up a large smooth pebble, and hurl it out over the water. It arcs through the air, contacting the sea with a splash, flashes of pure white and turquoise water sparkle in the sunlight. The pebble disappears into the depths below. My way of letting go of the past and looking forward.

*

We sit at the kitchen table, waiting for Mum to come home from work. My stomach twists with nerves because I know she's going to ask about the boat and the money and I can't lie to her. I just hope she buys into the story that the boat sale raised enough money to pay off her mortgage.

Before I even hear the front door shut, Mum's voice rings out, "Grandad, where's that bloody boat gone?" She steps into the kitchen, a puzzled look on her face, as she dumps a couple of shopping bags on the side. "Tell me that boat's gone for good, this is the first time I've managed to park my car on the drive for years. Tell me it's gone once and for all."

"I've sold it," Grandad declares, "So yes, it's gone for good."

"About time! How long have I been asking you to get that bloody boat off the drive?"

"Come and sit down with us Mum, we have something we want to give you."

She looks concerned as she pulls out a chair, glancing from me to Grandad. "What's this about? You two better not be in trouble?"

Grandad slides a box across the table with Mums eyes curiously following it. "This is a gift," he says, "Jus' our way of saying thank you for everything yew do for us."

Mum carefully opens it. Inside it is stuffed with cash. Her face freezes, and her eyes fill with disbelief. "How much is in here?" She whispers, her voice barely holding steady as she becomes very emotional.

"It's enough to pay off the mortgage and 'ave a holiday."

Mum's eyes well up, as tears slip down her cheeks. "Where did all this come from?" Her tone shifts, now suspicious, "And don't you think about lying to me, I can read you both like a book."

"The sale of the boat," Grandad replies. It's true enough, though we obviously had to add a little more.

She covers her mouth, sobbing softly. "I—I don't even know what to say." Her face a mixture of relief, joy, and love.

Watching Mum's reaction to the money confirms the boat sale was the right thing to do. I will certainly miss the boat and what it stood for, but Grandad pulled this one off and for all the right reasons.

Mum reaches for her phone, "I'm ringing Karen right now to tell her to start looking for holidays!" She dashes off, hearing the excitement in her voice as she calls Karen and announces 'its holiday time' was so lovely. I look over to see Grandad wiping his eyes discreetly whilst avoiding eye contact with me. We both just nod, that's all that's needed to confirm we've done the right thing and that's exactly what Mum deserves.

*

The climax of our secret mission comes to fruition, all our hard work, everything we've achieved, has led to our celebrational gathering. It plays out at Bottom Beach with local bands on makeshift stages showcasing their talent, food vendors from across the county fill the air with mouth-watering smells. Colourful tents, housing games bring laughter from both children and adults. It's amazing to see everyone together united and having such fun.

As I wander through the crowd, watching faces light up with joy, I pause, catching the soft sounds of a familiar voice. On a small side stage, Ruby performs. I've known Ruby since she was young and her voice captivates me every time I hear it. I find a resting place on the warm sand and drift into her melodies. The sun begins its slow descent toward the horizon, the sky transforms into a canvas of breath-taking hues, shades of crimson and gold bleed into the soft embrace of pastel pinks and purples.

How lucky are we to witness such beauty for free, it's only in the moment that you can truly find your happiness. We're all guilty of living in the past, or so far into the future that we forget to stop, look, and listen. Be still for a while. Take a moment for yourself, you always deserve it.

If you haven't yet visited Cornwall with your own eyes and smelt the sea air, then follow the A30 down into the magical kingdom of Kernow. When you see the trees up on the hill standing tall and strong in all their glory, remember you're almost there.

Lost in my moment, I'm startled when Alice jumps on me from behind. "Daydreaming again Beach Boy?" she asks.

"Lost in the moment as always."

She sits next to me and snuggles in to enjoy the beauty of Ruby's voice. Moments later, she asks, "What's next?"

"Not sure," I respond. "I have something for you though," I whisper with excitement.

"I also have something for you, but you first."

I reach into my bag and pull out a little box. "This is for you Alice. I want to thank you for being part of my life." I hand her the box to open. Inside is the Black Pearl I had kept from the treasure, the one item we all agreed we could have as a keepsake, "I've had it made into a necklace for you, I know how much you love pearls."

"It's so beautiful! Thanks Tim! Can you put it around my neck please?" I gently move her hair to one side and clasp the necklace in place.

"It suits you."

"I truly love it. Now my turn," she says, bouncing with excitement as she hands me an envelope with '**HOPE**' written on it. I open with care, and inside are two tickets. Instantly I notice bold letters spelling out 'Time to Travel' alongside a sunlit picture of Australia's coast.

"They're Plane tickets. I want you to see my home, my land, will you come on a new adventure with me, down under?" A mixture of nervousness and excitement sets in, I'm going to fly halfway around the world, and I've never even been on a plane before.

"Will you hold my hand?"

"Always, Beach Boy."

We head back to the café its alive with energy as the evening draws to a close. The celebrations have been a roaring success with laughter, clinking glasses, and the warmth of community filling every corner.

Karen comes bundling up with Mum, glasses in hand and slightly wobbly. She flings her arms around me and squeezes me tightly, "Thank you darling, your mum and I are off to Italy, it's all booked. I've always wanted to go and you've made it possible, you're an absolute angel. Ciao per ora!"

Amidst the buzz, Sam's a bundle of nerves; bouncing on the balls of his feet. Tonight's the night. He's been planning this moment for weeks and has been carrying the small velvet box in his pocket, itching to finally drop to one knee and ask Daisy to marry him. Meanwhile, Grandad stands near the door, a wistful look in his eyes. His bags packed, and soon he'll be leaving, setting off on a new adventure - driving to Scotland in Honey with Max. You can tell that he's itching to leave.

"Where's Dylan?" Sam mutters, pacing and scanning the room. "He was supposed to be here, where is he?"

Grandad leans in, his voice impatient, "Yew doin' this or wha' lad?"

Just then, Dylan bursts through the door holding

hands with Lydia both slightly out of breath. "Sorry, dude. Did I miss it?"

Sam lets out an exasperated sigh, "About bloody time, where've you been?"

We all gather close, sensing the significance of what's about to unfold.

Sam climbs onto a table in the middle of the café. Up there, under the warm glow of the hanging lights, he suddenly looks small and vulnerable. He clears his throat, trying to steady himself. He attempts to hush the crowd, but the chatter and laughter continue, oblivious to his presence.

Max, ever the commanding presence, rises to his full height and bellows, "can I 'ave yer attention yew lot? Listen up!"

The noise slowly dwindles, conversations trailing off into hushed murmurs until the room settles into an expectant silence.

Sam glances at Max for reassurance and he gives him a nod, "Yew got this, lad."

Taking a deep breath, Sam faces the crowd. "Thank you all for being here today, for celebrating with us, and for being part of this amazing community." Daisy's eyes widen in surprise. Public speaking is not Sam's thing, it never has been. She watches, intrigued and a little concerned, as he continues.

"There's something very important I need to say." His voice wavers slightly, but he presses on, "I've been so lucky to find my soulmate, the most beautiful woman I have ever known." Now looking directly at Daisy, "She's my everything, and I can't imagine my life without her."

A hush falls over the room as Daisy slowly steps forward, realisation dawning on her. Sam takes a deep breath. His hands tremble slightly as he reaches into his pocket and pulls out the small box. Then, right there on the table, he drops to one knee.

"Daisy," he says, his voice thick with emotion, "Will you marry me?"

A tear rolls down Daisy's cheek. The room is deathly silent, everyone holding their breath and waiting for her response.

Then, in a small but certain voice, she whispers, "Yes, Sam. Yes, I'll marry you. Of course, I will."

The café erupts into cheers, applause, and laughter. Sam grins, his hands unsteady as he opens the box and slides the ring onto Daisy's finger. Daisy starts to leap about, full of excitement and staring at her beautiful ring. Sam had it made especially with his keepsake from the treasure.

Alice leans in close and whispers in my ear, "One day, Beach Boy." She presses a soft kiss against my cheek. Dylan flings his arms around us both, pulling us in tight. "That'll be you two one day lovebirds." Alice gives him a knowing smile and giggles.

Daisy, overwhelmed by the moment, searches the room until her eyes land on Max. Over time, she has come to see him as a father figure, a steady presence in her life. Her real father lives near London, but they rarely see each other. It's Max she turns to now, flinging her arms around him as he lifts her off the ground proudly.

Max meets Sam's gaze over Daisy's shoulder, "Yew best look after this one while I'm away or yew'll 'ave me to answer to. Got it?"

Grandad steps forward, offering his hand to Sam. "Yew sure yew know wha' you're doin', lad?" He says, laughing, "She's a hand full, this one is."

Sam grips his hand firmly. "Never been surer Grandad."

He nods, his expression softens, "Well, I'm truly happy for yew both. Jus' don't get married until we're back. I love a good wedding, me."

As I watch them, I feel a lump rise in my throat.

With that, Grandad and max signal that they are heading off and make their way outside. We all walk towards the car park, where Honey is waiting to take them on their new adventure.

I walk alongside Grandad, "You take care now," He says, his voice gruff with emotion. "And promise to look after each other."

"I will, I'll see you when I get back from Australia."

Grandad stops in his tracks, turning to me with raised brows. "Australia? But yew've never even left Cornwall, lad! Wha' are you thinking? When are yew goin'? This is a surprise and a shock, yew go steady mind."

"Alice bought the tickets. We leave next month," I say, unable to hide my excitement. "I'll be back before Sam and Daisy's wedding, we're only going for six weeks. Can you imagine leaving them on their own to organise a wedding? Who knows what would happen! You old buggers better be back in time for that as well. Can't have a stag do and a wedding without the full crew!"

Grandad chuckles. "Don't yew worry, lad. We'll be back in plenty of time."

As we all gather around Honey to see them off, I take a moment to soak in the scene. The café lights illuminating the laughter and chatter of those I love most. Mum and Karen are a little tipsy, giggling like teenagers that are excited about their up and coming holiday. Dylan and Lydia are wrapped up in each other, whispering softly. Sam and Daisy beam with excitement, caught up in the magic of their engagement. Alice, standing beside me, squeezes my hand tightly. Then, out of the corner of my eye, I spot Mr Martin. He doesn't speak, he just nods, slow and deliberate, and I understand the unspoken words between us.

Max climbs into the driver's seat and turns the key. The old van wheezes, coughing out a tired groan before falling silent. He tries again and Honey rattles, then gives up completely. Grandad frowns, glancing at Max with concern.

Dylan, laughing, shouts, "Need a push you two?"

Max turns the key again and Honey suddenly stirs in to life, sputtering as if waking from a deep slumber. A puff of black smoke escapes from the exhaust, the head lights flicker on and off trying to find new life. The van lets out a shuddering growl before finally settling into a steady hum.

Max gives us a thumbs-up through the window. Grandad leans out and calls, "Yew lot behave while we're gone, don't start any new adventures without us! Duw genes Kernow, at least for now."

We wave as the van rumbles down the road. I watch as Honey disappears into the distance, its taillights glowing in the darkening sky and then slowly fading.

I feel strange, the thought of not having Grandad and Max around is stirring up mixed emotions. It's them leaving, it's the end of something amazing. A chapter closing, the story finishing, the end of something that has been truly amazing.

Life's complicated
the alterative ending

Chapter 1

Safe

Back at the yard Sam and Daisy sit together at the table. Fixated and trance-like, they separate the piles of precious treasure into smaller heaps. Sam's eyes are large and piercing, reflecting the glimmer of the beautiful gems. I sit back for a moment and become the observer, watching each person's different reactions within the room. However, my role as the observer brings concern. Sam's eyes are showing me a hint of something I've not seen from him before. Grandad and Max celebrating, separate themselves from the group. I look at Alice who's standing alone, we stare at each other for a while, knowingly, as if we're sharing the same thoughts and emotions. Alice's eyebrows drop into a frown, her face displaying a moment of thoughtful contemplation. No words are exchanged, but an understanding has been shared between us. Why this sudden change in atmosphere? The group seems fractured: Sam and Daisy, Max and Grandad, even Dylan's isolated himself. He's pacing up and down nervously. The old floorboards squeak as he wanders. He stops, staring at the treasure, his brow beaded with sweat. He looks overwhelmed with responsibility, with a blunt commanding tone, he asks, "Where are we planning on keeping all this then?"

Sam and Daisy, not willing to be parted from their newfound treasure, appear panicked by Dylan's comment, their expressions uneasy. Max walks towards an old, large, wall-mounted cupboard, all eyes following him with a sense of curiosity. At that same moment, in the corner of my vision, I'm distracted by a movement that has caught my attention.

I spot Sam's hand moving slowly, calmly but with intent. His movement direct and steady, aimed towards a small pile of gems he's placed near to himself. He picks up a handful, then slowly and calmly, retracts his hand back under the table, seamlessly. My heart beat's deeper and more pronounced in my chest. Did I just witness Sam stealing some of the treasure?

Max pulls open the doors of the cupboard, the wood creaks and groans as if waking from a long slumber, protesting the intrusion. Hinges stiff and unyielding from years of disuse emit a slow, rusty squeal that echoes through the room. Inside is a large, rusty, metal safe; shades of deep, burnt orange mingle with flecks of reddish-brown. Here and there, patches of dark, almost black corrosion contrast starkly with the rusty remnants of the original metal.

"In 'ere," Max says, looking back at us all. "We'll put it all in 'ere." Dylan, still pacing, stops, hands in his pockets and with a tightened posture, "But is that old thing secure enough? And who else has access to that safe Max?"

"Jus' me lad, I'm the only one with the key."

Dylan heads over to inspect the safe. He carefully looks all around it and even tries to pull it off the wall, testing its security. I notice Max and Grandad communicate, a slight side-to-side head movement demonstrating their disappointment and frustration in Dylan's actions.

"It'll be safe 'ere Dylan," Max says. "One key, and this old bugger's solid. No need to worry lad."

Dylan twists to face us all. "Don't you think it would be better to split it? Split it all up? We all take some to look after, so none of us holds the full responsibility. Imagine if the treasure got robbed. How would we all feel about that? I couldn't help but be suspicious if it suddenly went missing." Immediately, Max replies, his stance now intimidating, "Hang on therr, what 'ee fucking suggesting? No one's taking the treasure, yew don't trust me with it do 'yew Lad?"

"No Max, that's not it, I'm just saying we should all share the responsibility."

Grandad stands up to defend Max. "It's best kept 'ere, all together in one place, this is the safest place for it."

"I tell yew what lad, if you're tha' bloody worried about the treasure staying in my safe, and yew'm that paranoid I'm gunna steal it from 'ee," Dylan immediately interrupts Max, "I didn't say I was concerned about you stealing it Max, that's not what I meant."

"Well, you 'ave the fuckin' key then lad," Max walks

over to Dylan and abruptly shoves the safe's large key into Dylan's hand.

Max continues, his weathered face twisted in anger, "Tha' way we both share the fuckin' responsibility. It's my safe, in my yard, and you 'ave the key. It'll stay right 'ere until we 'ave a better plan to move it on." Grandad approaches Dylan and places a hand firmly on his shoulder. "After all son, we all want the same thing 'ere. We've worked so 'ard together, and look what we've achieved. We should be celebrating." Grandad heads back towards the table, pours rum into a mug, and hands it to Dylan. He lifts his own mug and clinks it with Dylan's to connect and diffuse the situation.

"It's settled then," says Sam. "The treasure will stay here, and Dylan, you'll have the key." Everyone pretends to be happy with this idea, and the atmosphere eases. I'm, however, stuck. Disconnected and lost within my own thoughts and feelings.

The celebrating continues for several hours with rum and the exchange of stories about our adventure, but an underlying tension remains present. I pick up a cigar from Max's stash and walk outside, I need some air. Alice follows me, and together we stand looking out to the sea. It's cold and the air's thick with a moist coastal drizzle; mizzle – a mist that clings to your skin. In the distance, a foghorn can be heard. The sound's haunting, echoing across the water like the call of a lost soul whilst the ghostly beam of the lighthouse cuts through the mist.

Not breaking my stare which is fixed into the distance. "I'm not sure Alice, I'm not sure what we've done?" A gentle quiet response, "We need to get out of here Tim. We need to talk." Her hand squeezes mine tightly.

On re-entering, Sam and Daisy are getting ready to leave. "We're off then, it's late, and I need my bed," says Daisy, as I nod in agreeance, "Grandad, you coming?" I ask, "Alice said she'll drop us home."

"No son, yew go on. I'm staying 'ere tonight with Max." This isn't unusual, they often stay at the yard after a session on the rum. "Can I grab a lift if there's one going please?"

"Sure Dylan," Alice responds.

We all watch Max open the safe and carefully place the treasure inside. Dylan locks the safe and we all leave together. Max opens the gates to the boatyard and immediately shuts them behind us. He puts a big padlock on, the clanking sound of metal on metal echoes in the mist as he wraps the chains around tightly and returns to the office. I watch his silhouette fade into the darkness.

Sam hugs me, it feels strange and I'm disappointed in him, so the hug isn't welcome. "We did it man," He says. Daisy hugs Alice and then Dylan. "What a day! love you guys." They both walk off in the direction of home and Daisy looks back, "Look after that leg Alice!"

Dylan jumps into the car with Alice and I. We're silent, each of us drowning in our own thoughts. The weight of what I'd witnessed presses heavily on my shoulders, the feeling that something terrible is unfolding. Dylan simply says, "Goodnight guys." As he opens the door and leaves the car. With the sound of the door slamming, Alice immediately looks straight at me and says, "What an evening, that was not what I was expecting."

Chapter 2

Questions and confessions

We both take a deep breath. "Let's go Alice."

"Where we heading?" She asks. "Let's drive to the point. Can't go home yet my heads buzzing." We head to the point, it's late, the air still thick with mist. As we arrive, other than a stealth camper, we're the only ones there. Alice turns the engine off, it's quiet for a moment then she asks, "What have we just witnessed? Did you see it?"

"See what?" I reply.

"Daisy, did you see Daisy? She took some of the treasure. She took some of it, Tim! I had to question myself at first, but I know what I saw, I saw it with my own eyes." Alice pauses and then continues, her tone lowered in disappointment, "I can't believe she would do such a thing."

Staring out into the darkness, "Sam did exactly the same thing," my voice hesitant, "He also took some."

"No! Really? Why? Why would they do such a thing?"

"As Max walked over to the safe, out of the corner of my eye, I saw him. I saw Sam take some treasure."

Alice grips the steering wheel tightly, her knuckles white. "What the fuck's happened?" Her voice trembling. I shake my head in disbelief, unable to explain the confusion and betrayal I'm feeling.

"Can you believe they've fucking stolen some of the treasure?" I slam my hands down onto the dash, fuelled by anger. "Shit, shit, shit, why? Why have they done this to us?"

"We trusted all of them Tim. Now what? What does this mean? What happens now?"

A moment of silence as we both contemplate what's just happened. I feel let down by the people I love, my mind darkens like the night itself. Alice shuffles in her seat to face me, "What about Max and Grandad? They were distant and they separated themselves from us tonight, don't you think? Their behaviour was definitely different."

"Yeah, when Dylan and Max were discussing the safe, Max looked at Grandad in a way that's left me wondering. It's weird, there was a connection between them - a knowing look. Alice, please tell me I'm paranoid and I'm overthinking."

"I saw the same Tim, that connection between them made me feel uneasy. You're not paranoid, cos I saw it too."

We both sink back into our seats and I ask her, "What was Dylan thinking, questioning Max like that about the safe? He seemed stressed and hesitant about leaving the treasure at the boatyard."

"It concerned me how aggressive Max became towards Dylan when he questioned him." Alice adds, "I've not seen that side to Max. Do you trust him?"

"I've no reason not to, but to be honest, other than being Grandad's best friend and my boss, who is Max really?" We continue to analyse the events that had unfolded that evening. Our family unit that we'd created, spent so much time with, built trust with, now shattered, has left me questioning everything.

"We can't forget what we've seen tonight, Tim. They took some of the treasure, treasure that belongs to us all."

"We need to think about this carefully Alice. We can't react on emotion, this could become complicated very quickly. It's late, let's sleep on it."

*

The next morning, I sit in the kitchen alone with my thoughts, wondering about the people I love. The early morning light is low and soft, casting long shadows. My mind's confused and I'm tired, I didn't sleep at all. I'm naturally suspicious of everyone now. Last night's left me feeling annoyed and with so many unanswered questions. Why did they take some treasure? What were they thinking? Why did Max and Grandad separate from the rest of us? And Dylan seem so sketchy about who was looking after the treasure and where it was staying?

I've learned throughout my life not to fully trust all my thoughts, our brains are complex things designed to confuse, over-analyse and disorientate. However, I've come to recognise and trust that feeling, that intuition in the pit of my stomach. Something doesn't feel right at all.

My phone lights up.

Alice: *Morning wonderful human, how did you sleep? Have you heard from Sam?*

Tim: *Not well, my head's been spinning. How about you, you ok? No, I've not heard from Sam yet, why?*

Alice: *The café's shut!*

A cold shiver grips me, Shut? It's never shut.

I Sit wondering why the café shut. Seems strange, naturally I'm worried so I message Sam. He's Pissed me off but he's still my mate after all and I need to check he's ok.

Tim: *Everything okay dude?*

No reply. I message Daisy, no reply.

Tim: *They're not replying Alice, something's wrong.*

Alice: *Where are you?*

Tim: *At home.*

Alice: *I'll be with you in half an hour.*

I message Dylan.

Tim: *Have you heard from Sam or Daisy?*

Dylan: *No, why?*

Tim: *The café's shut and I've messaged them both, but no response.*

Dylan: *Where are you man?*

Tim: *At home.*

Dylan: *I'm on my way.*

Then, a message comes through from Sam. Part of me doesn't want to read it but I see the message starts with. "*I'm so sorry Tim*". Now I'm committed to read on.

Sam: *I'm so sorry Tim. We've done something wrong, really wrong. We need to talk to you, where are you?*

Tim: *At home Sam.*

Sam: *We're on our way.*

I'm confused about how I feel, I'm not sure I'm ready to face them both yet. What am I going to say? Why are they coming here and what do they want to talk about?

Dylan lives close, and soon he's peering through the kitchen window. He walks in with a concerned expression, "Where's Sam bro? It's strange, he never shuts the café."

"He's messaged now and they're on the way."

"They're coming here, why?" he asks.

"I think we're about to find out mate." I pour him a tea, and we sit waiting. I'm left questioning whether I should tell him about their betrayal before they arrive. I'm concerned Dylan would lose his shit, so it stays with me for now. Alice arrives, finding us both sitting at the kitchen table.

"Dylan, what are you doing here?" she asks.

"They're on their way."

"Oh, okay, this could be interesting." Alice's face expressing apprehension as she pulls up a chair to join us. My eyes meet hers signalling, *I'm feeling the same.*

Sam appears with Daisy. His eyes sunken, and his postures weak, whilst Daisy's hiding behind him as they walk into the kitchen. Sam reaches into his bag, hands trembling, head down and avoiding eye contact. He pulls out a neatly wrapped cloth. Carefully, he places it on the table, revealing the treasure they had taken last night. He sits to join us and Daisy stands behind him, as if to protect herself, scared of what was to come. Neither says anything, they just sit waiting.

"Okay, so what's this all about?" Dylan asks. "Why's there treasure here?" He looks around at us all searching for an answer, his voice, low and deep. Sensing his tone, Alice calmly says, "They took it last night Dylan." They both looked alarmed, realising that Alice knew all along. Sam rests his head in his hands with shame. Slowly, he looks up and says with a crackle in his voice, "We're so sorry guys. Truly, we are. I can't explain what came over us and why we did what we did."

Dylan, unaware they'd taken the treasure and shocked, pushes his chair back with force as he stands up, his face red and his fists clenched, "You took some! Why mate? What the fuck were you thinking? Were you planning on stealing it?"

"No Dylan," Sam responds. Daisy, gripping Sam's shoulders tightly, steadying herself while tears cascade down her face. Sam takes a deep breath preparing to respond.

"I saw you do it mate," I say. "Can you imagine what that felt like? I've trusted you all my life dude."

"I know Tim. That's why we're here. Your friendship means everything to us. We made a big mistake; please can you forgive us?"

Dylan, pointing his finger shouts, "No, fuck you dude! I can't get my head around this, I'm going outside for a rolly."

"Give him a minute, let him adjust, let him catch up."

"Did you really see me take it?" he asks.

Dylan marches back in. "That's right! That's why you're both here. You panicked, thinking you'd been seen, you knew they saw you. That's why you're here. You had no fucking choice but to own up!"

"Please, we don't know what came over us. We wouldn't be able to live with ourselves, so here we are, hands up, and honestly, that's it. We love you all so much. It's as simple as that dude, trust me."

"You going to tell Max and Grandad?" Daisy asks.

"Fucking right we are," replies Dylan.

Alice calmly says, "They don't need to know."

Dylan sits back down at the table. One thing about him is that he tends to explode but soon calms down. "I'm so glad you owned up to this Sam," I say. "I've been battling with this one all night." Dylan looks directly at Sam. "This better be all of it, you little shit." Then laughs and punches him in the arm as a way of forgiveness. "What were you thinking dude?" Daisy sighs with relief and moving from behind Sam, she joins us at the table. A little shaky, she looks up and says, "We're truly sorry guys." Wiping the tears from her cheeks, "What's going to happen to it all? Could we not talk to Mr Martin? He could be the one to help us sell it."

"Daisy you genius! How the hell did we not think of that sooner?" Dylan mutters.

"Let's talk to the old boys tonight, see what they think," Alice replies.

Chapter 3

Keys

Walking down to the boatyard, the late afternoon sun highlights the beauty of our colourful cottages in narrow cobblestone streets. Flower pots bloom with bursts of colour. As we pass Mr Martins, I glance through the window and notice the shop's empty. Sam and Dylan are mucking about, pushing each other. It's good to see them back to normal. Approaching the boatyard, its quiet, just the distant clinking of rigging against masts could be heard in the gentle breeze. Dylan's the first to reach the big metal gates and he shouts back, "It's locked!" Alice looks at me with a confused expression. Sam starts to shake the gates with frustration, looking back at us he asks, "Why's it locked? Where are they, they're meant to be here, has anyone heard from them today?"

"I'll ring Grandad." Somethings odd. I dial Grandad's number and it goes straight to voicemail. Sam immediately rings Max, but again straight to voicemail. I look at the others, not sure what to say or do next. Dylan breaks the silence. "Those two old buggers better not have done a runner with our treasure." Sam laughs, playing the comment down. "No, there must be an explanation," He says, "Funny how both their phones have gone straight to voicemail though, don't you think?" Daisy replies.

We sit on the grass waiting, but I can't sit still, I'm restless and start pacing.

"Ring Sadie," Alice suggests. "Yeah, ring Sadie," Dylan agrees. "If anyone knows where Max is, she will."

"Sadie, have you seen Max today?" I ask.

"No but he rang me this morning. Why Tim, what's wrong?"

"We're at the boatyard, and it's locked. There's no sign of Max or Grandad."

"Max has gone away, that's why it's locked up," she confirms.

"Did he mention Grandad?"

"No, but they were together last night, they both stayed at the yard."

"Strange. I've tried calling them both, but it goes straight to voicemail."

"You know Max, he's crap with phones, he never answers it. Send him a message, perhaps? As for Grandad, maybe he's gone with him?"

"Maybe, but he'd normally let me know. It just seems strange."

"Could we borrow your keys, Sadie? We left something in the office last night and need to pick it up."

"Sure, can you pop round though? Mum's out, and I can't leave my little brother."

"Thanks Sadie."

"Where are they?" Dylan asks.

"Not sure, but Sadie had a call from Max this morning to say that he's had to go away."

"What about Grandad?"

"No sign of him, but she said he may have gone with Max."

"You have the key to the safe though Dylan, right?"

"Yeah," reaching into his pocket he pulls out the key.

"Sadie said we can have her keys to the yard and office."

"Let's go then," Sam grabs Daisy's hand pulling her up off the grass and starts marching up the road. Alice hangs back. "You okay?" she asks.

"Something's not right, I just know that something's not right. I've got that gut feeling."

Sadie's house is up a steep hill about a twenty-minute walk away. Sam's on a mission and sets the pace. Dylan, trying to keep up, looks back at me and Alice. "I'm messaging them both right now. This is weird, they said they'd be there tonight, they're meant to be guarding our treasure."

"I'll ring Mum!"

"Mum have you seen Grandad?" I ask.

"No, but when you see him, tell him he's in trouble. He's meant to have mended that bloody gate today, and he hasn't. I haven't seen him all day."

We pick up the keys and head back to the yard. Dylan's inventing possibilities, his imagination's running riot as he considers what may have happened. Sam contributes, not really helping the situation, "As long as the treasure is still there, those old buggers can do what they like." Alice squeezes my hand, preparing me for what might be coming next.

We return to the yard, unlock the gates and make our way to the office. The light is fading as dusk settles. Dylan shoves the door, revealing a dark and empty room. He switches the lights on and they flicker on and off for a moment. The room's quiet and cold. "Well, they're definitely not here! What the fuck do we do if it's gone?" Sam asks. "It's not gone Sam," I say, walking over to the safe. Dylan joins me holding the key and we both look at each other, his eyes are wide with apprehension. He puts the key into the rusty lock and turns it gently. But suddenly stopping, he says, "It'd better be in here." The hinges grate with age and rust as he slowly opens the door.

It's empty, it's all gone. I look at the others, searching for answers or some form of reassurance. Blank faces stare back at me and I feel faint with disbelief as my mind grapples for logic and reason. I glare back into the darkness of the safe, double-checking my eyes are telling the truth. Dylan, kicks out at a chair. "They've fucking robbed us all." Daisy, motionless, and with sadness in her eyes, walks over to Sam who's fallen to his knees and is holding his head in his hands. She comforts him by rubbing his back, staring at us all. The room's closing in as the reality sweeps through us.

I stagger over to Alice for a hug. "You're shaking," she says. "Why, why have they done this?" I ask. I feel the tears as they slowly run down my face. A familiar feeling of abandonment consumes me.

Sam gets to his feet stumbling back over to the safe, seeking confirmation. Turning now in Dylan's direction. "You're the only one with the key, Dylan where's the treasure?"

Dylan, pushes him in the chest with force. "Fuck you Sam. Fuck you, mate. I've not taken it. This has nothing to do with me. You're a fine one to talk anyway, so fuck you."

"Where's it gone then?" Daisy asks, defending Sam.

"How the fuck do I know? But obviously there's more than one key!"

"Leave it, just leave it!" Alice shouts, "We need to think this through, together calmly."

Dylan, now defensive, shouts at Sam, "I have the key, but only to the safe. I don't have a key to get into the boatyard you knob, nor do I have the key to get in here. So, no, I haven't taken the fucking treasure, so you need to get that into your thick head mate."

"Dylan's right, he hasn't got access to the yard, so he couldn't have taken it. That's not what's happened here Sam." I try to reassure.

Alice diffuses the situation, lowering her voice, "Listen, this is a shock for us all. No one expected it not to be here and none of us know what's happened or where it's all gone. There's nothing we can do tonight. We need to track down Grandad and Max, and hope they know where it is and that it's safe. Perhaps there is a logical explanation. Let's all just head home and wait. Let's give it until tomorrow, and hopefully, we'll hear from them."

We lock the yard up. Alice and I return the keys to Sadie and head back to her place for the night.

*

It's late as we arrive at Alice's house, her parents are asleep. We softly make our way upstairs so as not to disturb them. Alice shuts her bedroom door with a soft click, lights some candles, and burns incense to try and create a calm environment. I sit, consumed by the evening's events. The gentle light from the candle's flickers around the room whilst the perfume of the incense helps me feel more relaxed. I lie on Alice's bed and she joins me. Together we quietly talk through the chain of events, sharing our thoughts.

"What are we going to do?" I ask Alice.

"Nothing we can do at the moment, we just have to wait. Either Max and Grandad have taken it for themselves, or they've taken it to sell it and haven't told us."

I rest my head on Alice but suspicion and paranoia's taken a hold. I even run through the possibility that Sadie and Dylan have worked together to steal the treasure for themselves, they both have the keys after all. But that didn't explain the disappearance of Max and Grandad. My head's working overtime. Dylan could have double-crossed us, but he's not some kidnapper or murderer, that's for sure. Everything points to Max and Grandad. It was their mannerisms when they separated themselves from the group, that raised suspicions for me in the first place.

"What do we know about Max?" Alice asks.

"Not a lot. He's been in all our lives forever, he owns the boatyard and has a house on Quarry Hill, but that's it."

"Does he have family?"

"Not that I am aware of"

"What about his nature? You've worked for him. What's he like?"

"He's grumpy and thinks the world owes him, always moaning and thinks everyone else is better off than him. He's been good to me though."

"What about Grandad?" Alice continues.

"Ever since I lost Dad, Grandad's been there for

me. He's been everything I could have asked for. I love the fella inside and out." I pull my memories to the forefront of my mind, looking for any signs, anything that could be wrong and makes no sense. We continue to talk until I notice Alice has fallen asleep. She looks at peace so I blow out the candles and cuddle into her.

*

Two weeks pass and there's still no sign of Grandad or Max. The boatyard feels emptier with each passing day, it's quiet without Max whistling and barking orders. I sit in the office alone and stare at the empty safe, the air's thick with unanswered questions.

Sadie and I continue to look after the yard, as Max remains elusive. His phone's now off, and his house shows no signs of life at all. Dylan makes daily visits, even talking to the neighbours, but no one's seen or heard from him. Mum isn't overly concerned, as Grandad has disappeared for weeks at a time before. However, she knows nothing about the missing treasure. Perhaps she'd think differently if she knew. I've also noticed that Mr Martin's shop has remained shut ever since we found the treasure. Is this just a coincidence?

In the third week, a man turns up at the yard. He's young, smartly dressed, and holding an iPad. I'm cleaning one of the boats while Sadie sorts through some old nets that have seen better days. "Hello!" He shouts looking around. Sadie stops what she's doing and walks over to him.

"Can I help you?" she asks.

"Yes, are you Sadie?"

"Yes, I'm Sadie. What can I do for you?"

"I'm Jake from Harrington and Sons Estate Agents." I watch him pull out his business card, I put down my bucket and walk over to join them. "Estate agents?" Sadie asks.

"I've been instructed by the owner to complete an evaluation as the yard is going up for sale."

Sadie looks directly at me confused. "For sale?"

"Have you seen Max?" I quickly ask.

"Max?"

"The owner. We haven't seen him for weeks, and we're naturally concerned."

"No, I'm afraid not. We've had correspondence but not face to face. I'm here to complete the valuation. The owner's instructions are that it enters the market as soon as possible."

"What about us?" Sadie asks.

"The owner has mentioned nothing about employees."

"When's it going on the market?" I ask.

"As soon as I've completed the evaluation and taken some photos. It'll go up along with his house sale. I'm heading there straight after this."

"What? he's selling his house as well?" Sadie asks.

"That's the instructions I have, were you not informed of this?"

"No, we haven't had any contact for weeks now."

"Sorry guys, I'm just doing my job. Do you mind if I have a look around and take some shots?"

Jake walks off, taking photos. Sadie and I exchange bewildered looks, the weight of uncertainty pressing down on us. "Sorry Sadie, this is as much of a shock to me as it is to you."

I message Alice and Dylan.

Tim: *Meet me at Sam's later.*

When I arrive at Sam's, Dylan is sitting outside, a look of concern etched on his face.

"What's up?" he asks. Alice, Sam, and Daisy join us almost immediately.

"Max has instructed that the yard and his house be put up for sale. A man from Harrington and Sons Estate Agents came to the yard today."

Silence, followed by a barrage of questions. Sam's the first to speak, his voice trembling with rage, "They planned this, didn't they? The pair of them planned the whole thing."

"It may seem that way Sam," I say.

Daisy, is pacing aggressively, fuelling Sam's rage, and sarcastically says, "Get the youngsters to do all the work and then rob them, that was their plan."

"I can't believe they've done this to us, the pair of fucking shitheads," Sam says, anger blazing in his eyes.

I'm sat alone, looking into the sand, lost in my own thoughts and not wanting to listen. I look up to Sam and say, "You've lost your share of the treasure mate, but we all have. I've also lost my Grandad, think about that Sam, just for a minute yeah!"

Sam sits alongside me, "Sorry mate." He wraps his arm around me. "You okay, bro?"

"Like you Sam, I'm pissed off and angry. But he's still my Grandad and I'm worried about him. We've had no contact at all, and yes, we're assuming he's had a part to play, but we don't really know, do we?"

"I think we bloody know what's happened here," Daisy says, walking off." They've fucking robbed us all."

*

That night I ask Mum if she's heard from Grandad. The house feels different without him. The usual chaos has been replaced by a quietness and an emptiness. Mum carries on as if nothing is wrong. Keeping herself busy, I now understand, is her way of coping with stress.

"Are you okay?" I ask. "Yes." Mum avoids eye contact as she's tidying up an already tidy house. She's holding something back, I can sense it.

I tell her about the estate agent visiting the yard and that Max's house and yard are going up for sale.

She finishes wiping the worktops, flops the cloth in the sink and joins me at the kitchen table.

Mum looks tired, her voice quiet as she says, "I've no doubt whatever's going on, they're in it together. Where your Grandad goes, Max has always followed and vice-versa."

I sit looking at Mum, perhaps I should tell her about the treasure, but I hold back because it's not the right time. "One thing you need to know about your Grandad is that he's always done what he wants, regardless. You think he cares when actually he's as selfish as they come, he's only ever cared about money and what he wants to do. Stubborn and selfish, just like his father."

"Mum, is this why Nan left because of him? I can't remember Grandad being that sad or worried about Nan leaving."

"Tim, that whole situation is far more complicated than you will ever know. He didn't care Tim, he was glad to see the back of her. Never did he mention her, it was as if she'd never been a part of his life, he just carried on as normal."

"Where is she, Mum?"

"Who?" Mum replies, as if deflecting the question. She gets up from the table and walks over to the kettle, "Tea?" She asks, flicking the switch whilst looking out into the garden lost in her own thoughts.

"Nan?" I ask.

Mum carries on preparing the tea and rustling up

some biscuits. I sit back, watching her. This pause in our conversation seems an obvious break to allow mum to prepare for what she wants to say next. The spoon clinking on the china mug as she stirs is loud. Mum gathers her thoughts. I watch her hand slightly shaking as she places the tea and biscuits onto the table. "When Nan left, she asked me to promise her a couple of things. But if I tell you Tim, you must promise not to say anything to anyone." In a louder more assertive voice, "Now promise." She demands. "Ok, I promise."

"Your Nan asked me to keep in touch with her, which I've done."

"Hold on! So, for all these years you've been in contact with her?"

"Yes, she's my Mother-In-Law Tim, after all."

"I'm confused," I say.

"Well, let me finish and maybe you won't be. She made me promise to stay in touch because she wanted to know how you were doing. She needed to know you were okay. She's always been interested in how your life was developing. She was super excited when I told her about Alice. She's always said you would make the best boyfriend or husband and she prayed that you would meet someone special who loves you."

"So, she knows about Alice?" I ask.

"Yes, she was over the moon that you had found love in your life."

"How do you talk?" I ask, realizing that's a stupid question.

"On the phone," Mum responds, "we catch up on all the gossip every week. Nan's recently bought a smart phone so we can video call now and its lovely to see her face."

"So why haven't I been included in this? It's been so many years, I've not had any contact, I've not even seen her. Why haven't you told me before. Where's she living is it close?" I ask.

I feel pushed out, confused as to why I've not been included. All this time Mum's been hiding this from me, why?

"When she left, she moved to Somerset."

"Have you been?"

"Yes," Mum says.

"This is mental," I respond. "Is she okay? What's her house like? Is she happy? Is she well?"

"Slow down," Mum responds. "When she left, she made me promise to keep in touch but never to let Grandad know where she was and it would be our secret. It's been hard Tim, but I made that promise. I needed to keep her in my life."

"So, when have you been up to see her?"

"Once a year I go to see an old friend, right? None of you've ever asked, so it's been easy. One week every year I go and stay with Mum. We have a good catch-up. She's made a great circle of friends and we have a lovely time together. When she left, she made me promise not to tell you where she was. This was the hardest thing I've had to do. It was difficult because I felt I was going behind your back, and it never sat well with me Tim. However, she also made me promise that when the time was right, I was to give you her address. I never thought it would come, but I am now guessing this is the time."

Mum gets up and walks towards the cupboard under the stairs. After rummaging around she brings back a small notebook and grabs a pen, and starts writing. "This is Nans address," She says, and slides it over in my direction.

"I have so many questions," I say.

"Well, maybe this is your moment to find your answers." Mum replies. "Tim, what you seek though may not be what you wish to know, be mindful of this before you make your decision to speak with her."

"Will you ring her and arrange for me to go and see her?" I ask.

"Yes, if that is what you truly want Tim." Mum replies.

Chapter 4

Reunited

Later that evening, Alice and I head to Bottom Beach. We sit close to the water's edge; gentle waves roll in as we watch the last threads of sunlight touch the water. I start to tell Alice about the conversation I'd had that afternoon with Mum. But before I get into the details, I receive a message from Mum.

Mum: *I've spoken to Nan, when do you want to go to see her?*

"Sorry Alice, I just need to check something." I look up trains to Somerset and see an early morning one tomorrow. I message Mum back,

Tim: *Tomorrow?*

A moment later, Mum responds:

Mum: *That's fine. She's expecting you.*

I immediately book a return ticket for 8:05am in the morning, and then I bring Alice up to speed, and she's as shocked as I am with Mums disclosure.

"So, are you happy to meet her?" Alice asks.

"Yes, I feel that I need to. I've so many questions."

"Well, let me drive you one day," Alice says.

"Thanks for the offer, but I've just booked my train for 8:05am tomorrow morning."

"Well, you didn't hang around there Tim." She says with a small chuckle, "How do you feel?"

"Nervous, but excited to see her again, it's been such a long time. One of Mum's comments this afternoon freaked me out a little, she said I might not like all the answers to my questions. I still have to go though, I want to see her, she's my Nan."

"Well, I'll pick you up in the morning and drop you at the station." Alice leans in and gives me a big cuddle, full of warmth. "Good luck, Beach Boy, I hope you find the answers you're looking for."

My mind's full with apprehension and excitement, but what if Mum's right? What if the answers I seek only bring more questions?

*

On the train down to Somerset, my brain's buzzing. I try to imagine what Nan now looks like, the image in my head isn't clear as its been years, I wonder how she's changed. I search her address and decide to get a taxi, since she lives a little way from the station, I want to spend as much time with her as possible before I have to head home this evening.

I haven't left Cornwall in so long; the journey becomes my thinking time. The train rumbles beneath me, the rhythmic clatter filling the carriage. It sways gently, vibrations humming through the seat. I had forgotten there's a world outside my beautiful county. I mentally relive the past few months, walking through conversations and actions, trying to find a reason why Max and Grandad have disappeared, and why they've taken the treasure.

Staring out of the window at the Devon countryside, I am drawn to the beauty of the landscape. Rolling hills quilted in green patchwork, dotted with grazing sheep and vibrant wildflowers. Stone cottages nestle amidst vast fields, while dense woodlands weave in and out of view. The distant coastline occasionally peeks through, reminding me of home.

Time soon passes and at the end of the carriage, the sign illuminates my stop and the train comes to a gradual halt. I admire the stations rustic charm and character as I step onto the platform. I suddenly feel the nerves creeping back in. This is the moment I get to see Nan again after so many years. Leaving the station, it's drizzling with rain and it's cold. I grab a taxi, and we weave through the bustling streets, heading in the direction of Nan's house.

"What's it like here?" I ask the driver, trying to distract myself from the knot forming in the pit of my stomach.

"It's not like it used to be," she replied, her tone tinged with nostalgia.

"In what way?" I ask, sensing a story coming.

"It used to be small, like a community town, everyone knew everyone. Not no more, over the last few years it's grown bloody loads, them building houses everywhere, more and more people come each year and now it's lost that community vibe. You'd be able to walk up town and bump into all sorts, catch up on gossip and all that. Not no more though, I don't go in town, not really. No shops left, them all bloody gone, they are."

Arriving at the address, I stand for a moment to gather my thoughts, my stomach's still in knots. Nans house is pretty looking, a small terrace style on a quiet street. The area looks well-presented. As I walk towards the front door, the path's narrow and mature, well-tended plants and flowers soften the edges - guiding the way. Before I could knock, it opens. A lady much older than I expected and smartly dressed stands with the loveliest of smiles.

"Nan?" I ask.

"Tim," She reaches out with a welcoming hug. The smell of her perfume is so familiar and brings back memories that have been buried deep. "Come in my love, I've been expecting you."

The entrance presents a long thin corridor which leads to the kitchen. The kitchen door's slightly open. My attention is drawn to a peaked cap hanging on a hook, not something I imagine Nan wearing. She ushers me into her front room. "Sit down." She orders, moving some cushions to make room on the sofa. "How was your journey, love?" Before I could even answer, she continues, seeming nervous, she asks "Would you like a cup of tea?"

"Yes please, Nan."

She stops for a moment, standing directly in front of me and just staring, studying me. "Look at you, how you've grown since I last saw you. Your mum's shown me pictures, you're a handsome man, so much like your Dad." She broke her stare and walked off to get the tea. I was left alone in the room, my eyes searching for familiarity. Her front room's small, compact but homely. My attention's drawn to a photo on the mantelpiece. I walk over for a closer look. It's a photo of my Dad. A new set of emotions rush through me as I pick it up for a closer look. Mum had removed his photos from the house when he died, I guess her way of coping. I hadn't seen his face in so many years, he looks young and exactly as I remembered. I hear a slight rattle of china as Nan walks back into the room, her hands slightly shaking as she passes me a delicate cup and saucer.

"That's your Dad." Nan reaches out and takes the photo from me. She sits carefully, clutching the photo close to her chest.

"It's so lovely to actually see you again Tim, it's been so very long. How's Alice?" she asks. I immediately smile, hearing her name brings a warmth.

"She's fine, Nan."

"You're in love, I can see it in your smile. As soon as I said her name, you lit up."

"She's amazing!"

"Just what you deserve love."

"How are you though Nan? How've you been?"

"Nan!" She laughs. "No one's called me that for many years. I've been well, I'm very lucky, I'm surrounded by some lovely people. I moved into this very house when I left Cornwall and I've been here ever since. Betty's next door and we look after each other, she's not quite as active, but she's great company and loves a gossip."

"You're in good health, though?" I ask.

"Fine, I think it's being brought up with all that Cornish air, it's put me in good stead in my old age."

"Do you miss Cornwall?"

"Every day. Once you've been kissed by her, you'll never be the same. It's probably the most beautiful place in the world. I've been updated with all that's been happening."

"Well, I guess I'm playing catch up as I only found out yesterday that you've remained in contact all these years."

"We have my love." Nan says.

"Why did you leave?" I ask.

"Questions already?" She immediately stands up, "Don't you want cake first?" She hurries off in the direction of the kitchen again and returns with a plate of neatly sliced cake, placing it on the table. "Help yourself my love."

She sits on the edge of her seat, her posture's tense. "I've tried to prepare for this moment for years, going over what I would say when I saw you again. But seeing you face to face, well, it's a little harder than I thought it would be."

"It's okay Nan, I'm just pleased to see you."

"You have questions that deserve answers, you deserve to know my love, and I want you to know the truth." It seems as though she needs to get something off her chest. Her voice now commanding the room and demanding my attention reminds me of an old school teacher about to tell a story. I just hope I'm ready for this story. Before beginning she takes a deep breath and shuffles forward in her seat.

"Many years ago, Tim, there was a story about a ship that sunk just off our coastline, the ship had treasure on it. I know this to be true, it was all your Grandad's Dad, Stefan, used to talk about. I never took much notice, if I'm honest because it all seemed quite stupid to me. I kept out of it. Stefan was an angry man with very little patience. He had a map which he believed was drawn by the original fisherman, Tristan Richards. The map showed where the ship was to be found."

I sit, fixed on Nan's every word and listening intently. I was surprised that she knew about the treasure all along. I can't let on that I also know, so I try hard to keep my composure and eye contact steady.

She continues, "A few years after your Grandad lost his Dad, I had an affair. I thought I was in love. He was such a charming, thoughtful and kind man, unlike your Grandad, who was always full of mischief and never took life seriously. I became pregnant by this man, and as soon as I told him, he didn't want to know. He distanced himself, and not long after, he moved away. I knew what I had done was wrong, but at the time, I couldn't help myself. He told me he loved me and would be there for me and I believed him. Your Grandad and I went through a very dark time and very nearly parted. However, we agreed that we would keep it all a secret. No one knew about the affair, and despite Grandad's hatred towards the situation, he agreed to raise your Dad as his own. As time passed, things settled, and Grandad stood by his word. However, our relationship never recovered. There was no love left between us, and your Grandad never truly forgave me. Your Grandad was always convinced that one day he would find that bloody treasure. He turned the whole story into an adventure, talking with your Dad for hours about how they would one day find it and become rich. The pair of them became obsessed, it was almost like they kept it from me. It was their thing, their shared secret. It felt like I was being punished by your Grandad. He never included me, he never really included me in anything. They kept their stupid plan of treasure hunting a secret from us all. I know that day they went out together, that was what they were doing. I remember the feeling I had about the whole thing, it just didn't seem right, but there was no stopping them. When your Grandad returned home alone, I immediately felt the immense loss. I knew your Dad was gone, and gone forever. The pain was unbearable, and I blamed your Grandad for the whole thing. I fell apart. He was my true son, and it was as if Grandad had taken him away from me. I couldn't forgive him for that, I hated him. I had no choice but to leave so that's when I moved here. I needed to get away from him."

"Dads death was an accident though Nan." Her face is blank, emotionless and she says nothing in return but picks up the photo of Dad again, clinging onto it tightly. Her silence spoke a thousand words, and the atmosphere changes within the room. This is a new side to the story, one I'm not at all prepared for. Nan had an affair, so this meant Grandad was not my real Grandad. My mind races with this new revelation. The room feels smaller, the air thicker. Nan's eyes are distant, filled with memories and heartache that resonates off her. The ticking of the clock on the wall becomes louder, each second stretching out. I swallow hard, trying to process everything. How can everything I know about my family be so different from reality? This isn't just about treasure after all, this is about understanding the people I love and the choices they've made. I'm only just beginning to uncover the truth. Looking at her, I suddenly feel disconnected, as if I don't know this person that I'm calling Nan. Who is she really? She seems so unfamiliar to me now. She was clearly carrying guilt and anger, even after all this time. We sit in silence for a while as I try to make sense of it all. To break the uncomfortable silence, I ask "What was

Dad like?" Nan's mood switches and her face lights up, excited at the chance to talk about her son.

"He was a determined man with a kind spirit. Happy to help anyone and always smiling. We used to say he had ants in his pants because he couldn't keep still, not for a moment. Always doing something, some sort of project on the go. He loved you so very much Tim. I remember him taking you out on walks along the cliffs overlooking the bay. A true gentleman, he was."

This stirs up emotions I've buried deep. The moment Grandad told me about Dads accident flashes in front of my eyes, vivid and real. Becoming emotional and needing to change the subject quickly, I say, "Mum sends her love."

"She's done so well bringing you up on her own." Nan replies.

"Grandad did help as well," I add.

"I'm sure he did Tim, in his own way. Your mum tells me he hasn't been seen for a while though, I bet him and that Max have gone off on one of their adventures. He never changes."

"Did you believe there was treasure, Nan?" I ask.

She sits back and gathers her thoughts before responding. "Your Grandad's side of the family was convinced. That old map was passed down from generation to generation. I always knew there was no truth in any of it. Treasure? There was no treasure out there. It was just some made-up story. If there was treasure, don't you think someone would have found it by now?"

"Does Mum know Grandad isn't my real Grandad?" I ask.

"Yes Tim, she knows now."

"Did Dad know?" Nan pauses for a moment. She seems reluctant to answer but follows with "No, we never told him, because it felt like the right thing to do at the time." That sentence alone makes me feel so sad that Dad never knew the truth. I look up at the clock and realise how quickly the afternoon has passed. My train's due to leave soon. "I have to go shortly" I say. I feel somewhat relieved to be leaving as the room's been closing in on me and I feel the need to escape. My time with Nan has been interesting and certainly overwhelming, not what I expected. Mum warned me that I may find out things that could be difficult to understand and she wasn't wrong.

"Already? It seems like you haven't been here long." Nan saddened by my departure and with her head bowed slightly, says, "Perhaps you will come again and bring that lovely Alice with you. I would love to meet her."

"That would be nice, I'm sure Alice would love to meet you one day. I'll just call a taxi. Think's, Nan, for sharing this afternoon with me. It's been great to see you. Thanks for being so honest and letting me know about the history of our family. I appreciate how hard that must have been for you. There's a lot I need to process and take in. Do you know whatever happened to Dad's real father, my real Grandad?"

Nan, hesitant and nervous that I've asked the question, quickly stands up. Walking back towards the mantelpiece, she re-positions Dads photo in its original place. With her back turned away from me, she utters "No, I'm sorry Tim. I never saw him again." The image of the gentleman's cap I'd seen in the hallway flashes back into my mind. Curious, I ask, "What was his name?"

Nans voice soft, "Clive Thomas was his name, I really thought he was the one."

That name, Thomas, resonates with me, as if I know it from somewhere. So, I am a descendant of the Thomas family, not the Richards after all.

"The taxi's here Nan." Getting up from her chair, she walks over and hugs me. "Please come again Tim, it's been so lovely to see you. I appreciate this is a lot for you to take in, but you needed to know the truth."

I head to the front door, slowly turning to hug Nan one last time. I glance over her shoulder to see if the cap is real and I hadn't imagined it. It is still there. "It's been lovely seeing you again, take care." I walk down the path towards the car, but I don't look back.

"To the station please." I say as I sit in the back of the taxi, relieved I am out of that house. Mixed emotions run riot as we travel towards the station.

"How's your day been mate?" The driver asks.

With a deep breath in, I follow with, "Interesting."

The train's quiet, which suits me perfectly. It gives me time to unravel my backstory piece by piece and think through the information that Nan shared. She is an interesting person, not at all as I remembered. After all these years she certainly had a lot to say and keeping up with it all was difficult. I can't help but feel disconnected from her. I guess it's been such a long time and so much has changed. I was saddened in her presence, I felt her bitterness and her anger.

My mind sits uncomfortably, with a thought ignited by Nan's comment. When I mentioned it was an accident, she had no words, and I was left in silence wondering what to read into this. Did Nan think there was something more sinister at play? Or was that her way of driving a wedge between myself and Grandad? The fact that he's now gone leaves me thinking that I will never know the truth, and perhaps nor do I want to. I glance out of the window, it's raining and the speed of the train distorts my vision. Memories and flashbacks blur with the passing landscape. Tears swell in my eyes and slowly slip down my cheeks. 'Set him free, set Grandad free,' echoes in my mind.

I can now understand why she left but I'm struggling to quash the feeling of abandonment that comes with it. So, Grandad's not my real Grandad. That is the biggest shock and something I wasn't expecting. That newly gained knowledge, along with the realisation that we're probably never going to see the treasure or Grandad again, hits hard. The treasure, so be it, perhaps it was never really meant to be, but Grandad? I will never see that man again. A deep sadness fills my soul. What a man he's been, even knowing I was not his bloodline, he was always there for me. How hard must that have been for him? He was my constant throughout it all. Grandad was always there, never missing a moment to support me and guide me through life's challenges. For that, I will always be truly grateful. I will miss his words of wisdom and his quirky ways. I guess he lived his life the way he wanted to. All along, it seems he played the game and played it well. Maybe Nan's right to have her suspicions about him, maybe it wasn't an accident and maybe he'd planned the whole thing. I study drops of water as they trickle down the window. The dream of being deep in the ocean surfaces in my mind and the image of there being no boat freezes. Nans suspicions now making me paranoid. Perhaps Grandad didn't wait for Dad, perhaps it was no accident and Grandad's way of revenge. I break my focus from the image. I can't accept that Grandad would do such a thing. I make the choice whilst sitting there, that the suspicion, doubts and paranoia will not eat away at me, I can't allow it. I need to find some form of peace with the whole situation. My mind wonders back to the name Thomas. In reality, I'm a Thomas. As soon as she mentioned it, something inside me stirred and the name resonated deeply. Tracing a path back through my memories, I recall Grandad mentioning Tristan Richards and William Thomas when he was describing the note he'd found in the box along with the map.

The name Thomas keeps echoing in my mind. Can it really be just a coincidence? Or is there much more to this connection? The pieces of my family's history seem to shift and realign, creating a new, unsettling picture. As the train moves steadily towards home, I can't shake the feeling that I am on the brink of uncovering something monumental. Why was there a gentleman's style cap at Nan's? The name Thomas is no longer just a name; it is a key, a link to the past and had much more of a meaning now.

*

I arrive back at the station as dusk settles, the light's casting long shadows on the platform. There, under the dim glow, stands Alice, her presence a beacon in my turmoil. I get off the train and as I walk towards her, she envelopes me in a warm embrace and whispers, "I love you." I take a deep breath, inhaling her scent, grounding myself in that very moment. Despite all the lies, deceit, and loss, I believe her. I can feel it deep within.

In this moment, everything stops. My racing thoughts and the chaos of the past few months, all of it just stops. It's all irrelevant, everything is irrelevant. The only thing that truly matters in life is to feel genuinely loved, to have someone who believes in you, someone who stands by your side no matter what. Someone who walks alongside you, not ahead or behind, but by your side and someone who loves you for who you truly are, unconditionally.

Does anything else really matter? Maybe it's just that simple; maybe it's just being loved, and keeping hope close to your heart.

*

Months drift by and nothing's changed, there's still no sign of Max and Grandad. The boatyard's been sold and I'm currently searching for a new job.

    I've kept in touch with Nan with the odd phone call here and there. However, our relationship hasn't developed at all and she's still distant. Our conversations are hollow, filled with pleasantries and long silences. I had planned to visit her again with Alice, hoping that in some way, we could bridge the gap. Maybe, just maybe, she could help fill the void that Grandad had left behind. I wanted to try and build a better bond, but she's decided to move. Leaving her little house behind, she's moving to Spain. This has come as a surprise for Mum and I. Mum said that Nan had come into some money and decided to see her days out living by the sea again, but this time in the warmth.

    The weather here is dull, much like my mood. I head to the bench in search of something, some time to think. The whole situation has left me empty with more questions than answers. I can remember on the train ride home from Nan's that I told myself I would let him go, let Grandad go and not hold onto the anger I had felt towards him for taking the treasure and leaving us. I've tried to let the bitterness dissolve. He's gone, and holding onto anger wouldn't bring him back. But even now, despite every effort, I can't shake it. The past clings to me, refusing to let go. Things are so different without Grandad, there's an emptiness, the house is quiet and lifeless. More often than not I feel so alone, a feeling I've struggled with for most of my life. First Dad, then Nan and now Grandad. The darkness of the night begins to creep in, so I start to make my way back when my phone lights up with an unknown number and a message that reads:

Unknown: *I need to see you son.*

I burst into tears as this could only be one-person; Grandad. I hesitate in responding, a split feeling of anger and disbelief, yet an inner comfort that he's reached out at long last. The message leaves me confused, not knowing what to think or do, so I don't respond.

*

The house is quiet that evening, the glow of the television flickering across the room. Alice and I sit side by side on the sofa. My mind drifts, caught between the aching need to hear Grandad's voice again and the burning resentment that won't let me forgive him. That message - I wish I'd never seen it.

Alice shifts closer, resting her head against my shoulder. She doesn't say anything at first, just lets the silence settle between us. Eventually, she asks, her voice gentle, "What's wrong, Tim? You've been distant all evening. Are you okay love? I'm worried about you."

I exhale slowly, my fingers tightening around my phone before I slide it across to her. She picks it up, scanning the screen.

"Is this from Grandad?" She asks, sitting up straighter, the light from the phone casts across her face. "When did you get this?"

"Late this afternoon. It has to be from him." I rub a hand over my face, my mind's been so restless and I feel so exhausted. "But why, Alice? After all this time? What does he want? Why now?"

Softly, she responds, "So this is what's been weighing on you." She places the phone on the table and takes my hand. "Tim, bless you. How do you feel about it?"

"Confused." My voice a whisper, "Maybe angry, I don't know. But more than anything, I just want answers. I need to know the truth."

Alice squeezes my hand. "Then you have to respond. It's the only way you'll get any sort of closure." She hesitates, searching my face. "This whole thing has been tearing you apart. You're not yourself. I can see the sadness in you, and I get it, I do. You've never really talked about how it felt finding out Grandad wasn't really your Grandad. Maybe it's time, time to face this."

"Tim," She pauses for a moment, "Have you thought about trying to track down Clive? Maybe it would be good to have his side of the story to help you understand more."

"Where would I start? Nan said she hasn't seen Clive for years and I know Grandad hasn't had any contact. The only person I think has stayed in touch is Max and he's disappeared completely. Maybe this Clive doesn't even know he has a Grandson. After all, he left as soon as he knew he had a son, so I don't hold much hope that he's the sort of person I would want in my life any way. I have a Grandad and no one can replace him, I loved him so much Alice."

"Please Tim, message him back because he's reached out for a reason."

I stare into the low light of the candle, drifting through my thoughts and emotions. The buzz of the TV in the background adding to the scrambling within my mind.

I pick up my phone and start typing the words before flinging it back onto the table and sinking into the sofa, "I can't, I can't do it. I just need time."

I lie awake most of the night drifting in and out of restless sleep. I look at the clock and its 5.30am, Alice is fast asleep and looks so peaceful. I look at her and realise that I've been so preoccupied recently, I've distanced myself from the one person that's still here right by my side. I gently pull back the duvet, careful not to disturb her and grab my phone. I read the message again and I begin to write:

Tim: *Grandad, where are you? what's going on?*

I turn to get back into bed when a message comes straight back.

Grandad: *Will you come and see me, I need to see you Tim?*

Tim: *Where are you?*

Nothing comes back so I wait for a while.

Grandad: *I'm in hospital son.*

Tim: *Hospital? is everything ok?*

Grandad: *I can explain all if you are happy to come and see me. Please this is important I need to see you.*

Tim: *Grandad where are you, What hospital are you in?*

Grandad messages back the name of the hospital. I sit on the edge of the bed and Alice stirs, noticing me sat staring at my phone.

"Tim, you ok? What are you doing?" She asks. I get back under the duvet, still clutching my phone. "He's in hospital Alice."

"Why, why is he in hospital?"

"I don't know but I have the address."

"Then we need to go Tim, we need to go now!"

Alice agrees to drive me there straight away so we quickly get dressed and ready to leave. In the hour it takes to get there, we go back and forth trying to work out what's wrong with him and why he's ended up in hospital.

Walking towards the ward, I stop and turn to Alice. "Is this the right thing to be doing?" I ask. "Yes Tim, we must see him."

"Alice, should I tell him that I've seen Nan and I know he's not my real Grandad?"

"I think we play that one by ear, allow him time to explain. Let Grandad do the talking and hopefully you'll get the answers you need. But Tim, you need to be ready. He's in here for a reason, something is obviously wrong with him. You're going to need to be strong."

At the far end of the ward, tucked away from the bustle of nurses and the steady murmur of distant conversations, was a dimly lit room. The name on the door reads *Charly Richards*. My stomach tightens as we approach.

Through the slight gap in the curtain, I glimpse Grandad. Lying still in the bed, surrounded by machines that beep and hum, their lights blinking. Thin tubes snake from his nose and arms.

Alice grips my hand, her fingers laced tightly through mine, and she gently knocks on the door. We step inside. The walls, a pale shade of blue, seem to close in around us as we enter. A small window lets in a sliver of morning light, but it does little to soften the stark reality before me.

Grandad looks so different, unrecognisable, the sight was shocking and made me feel sick. He's frail, shrunken, his once strong hands now resting limply against the stiff hospital sheets. His skin's pale and drawn. I look over at Alice, who's now fighting back the tears. Then, slowly, his head turns towards us. His eyelids flutter but his eyes are sunken. For a moment, I see a spark of recognition.

"Tim, Alice... is that yew?" His voice is rasping, as he musters a weak smile. "Come, sit with me."

A lump rises in my throat as I step closer. Alice squeezes my hand once more, and together, we sit beside him. He reaches out and I grab his hand tightly, it's cold to touch and weak to hold.

"Thanks for coming. I needed to see yew both and explain."

"Explain what Grandad?"

"Everything son."

This was the worst thing I could be faced with, this is not the man I expected to see. This is the final stages of his life, I think to myself as I try to adjust.

"I didn't take the treasure Tim." Grandad splutters. He shuffles in his bed, trying to sit more upright. Alice supports him by moving his pillows, enabling him to be in a more comfortable position.

"Pass the water son, will yew?"

I pour a glass and hand it to him. His grip's so weak and his hand is shaky.

"How are you Grandad?" I ask. Clearing his voice, he looks in my direction, "I've been better son but therr's no time for tha', I'm just so glad yer 'ere. Tis so lovely to see you both. Has ee been looking after yew, Alice?"

"He has Grandad, you don't have to worry about that."

"How long have you been in here for?" I ask.

"I lost track of time son, but it feels like forever. I've been going mad in this little room, stuck in this bloody bed. I'm an outdoor sort of fella, yew know me, can't sit still for long."

"They've been looking after you though yeah?"

"They've been lovely, all the staff are great. I've got a soft spot for young Linda though, she's my favourite. Last week she even slipped a little rum in me water. Now listen yew two, this is important. Leading up to our adventure, I hadn't been feeling great. I kept it to meself, dint wanna worry anyone. I thought it would go away but it didn't. I was so caught up in all the excitement and wasn't going to miss us finding tha' treasure for anything. We did it, dint we?"

"We did Grandad!"

"That night, whilst Max and I was looking after the treasure at the boatyard, he seemed different and something didn't feel right. Max is complicated and not easy to read, he's always been an awkward bugger. Even back in the early days when it was us two and Clive."

I saw Alice glance over in my direction, her face startled as soon as Grandad mentioned the name Clive.

"I just wanted to sell tha' treasure, son," His voice raw with exhaustion, "Get the money, get yew and yer mum sorted and then I was going to see the doctor. Find out what was wrong and get meself fixed up and tha'." He exhales heavily.

"But bloody Max started acting differently, edgy. Even his laughter grew forced, his glances sharper and more guarded. I'd catch him on the phone, his voice low, muttering words I couldn't make out, and discussing something ee didn't want me to hear. Something didn't feel right. As we sat therr together drinking rum, the door to the office swung open, and in walked Clive.

The sight of tha' man made me angry. I hadn't seen him in years. It made no sense, why was he 'ere? Until I turned to Max and saw the way he didn't flinch, the way his expression remained blank, then it hit me son. This wasn't a coincidence. Max had been expecting him. They had kept in touch all these years, plotting something I had been too blind to see."

Grandad repositions himself, now looking more uncomfortable as he tries to piece together the next part of the story.

Sensing his pain and his discomfort, I say, "Grandad you don't have to, rest if you need."

"No Son, this has to be spoken about and yew need to know the full story. Yew need to know the truth. I'm not your real Grandad, Son." He pauses for a while, gathering his thoughts. This clearly was so difficult for him to say. I sit quietly, allowing him the time to continue.

"Clive's yer Dads real father not me. The bastard left as soon as he found out, leaving me to pick up all the pieces. Later, when yer Dad died, yer Nan blamed me and said tha' I had killed him because ee wasn't mine and tha' I had planned the whole thing. Yer Nan is riddled with guilt, she's not a nice lady son, she's twisted. I need yew to know tha' I didn't kill yer Dad and tha' it was just an accident. Despite him not being my Son, I loved him and would have never of let anything happen to him. That I promise to yew. At yer Dads funeral, he turned up, tha' fucking Clive. I wondered how ee knew and now it's clear that Max had told him. Yer Nan moved away after the funeral and started a new life with Clive." A flash back of the gentleman's cap at Nans rushes through my mind and a moment of realisation. So that was Clive's cap!

"When we decided to start looking for tha' treasure again, I now know tha' max kept them both updated. They had turned him against me. Tha' night in the boatyard, I saw the real Max.

They took the treasure and robbed us all. The three of them had it all planned out and was just waiting for the right time. I'm not sure, but I reckon tha' Mr Martin's involved somehow as well. When I saw Clive a rage of anger took over me and I went to punch him but I lost my footing and fell, crashing my head on the table. I hit the floor hard and was in a bad way. I could feel the sensation of blood trickling down my face as I lay there. My vision blurred, but I watched them both take the treasure. I heard Clive say 'just leave him' but Max bundled me into the car and dumped me off here at the hospital and that's the last I've seen of them.

They ran loads of tests, and told me I had cancer. Ive been here ever since. They say I only have weeks or even days left to live. That's why Linda helped me message you. I needed yew to know everything, I needed to see your face before I die, before it's too late." Suddenly, Grandad stops, no more words. A silence in his eyes as his head finds its final resting place on the pillow. There and then, his breathing becoming erratic. Alice now crying, knowing what was about to happen leans over and hugs me tight. He takes one more shallow breath until no more and we watch his life fade away. One tiny moment of silence until sounds erupted from the machines supporting him.

Nurses and doctors come flooding in, taking over and ordering us to leave the room. We watch from the window as they frantically try to save him but it was too late, Grandad was no longer with us. Moments after the chaos had settled, a young nurse approaches and asks if I was Tim. She introduces herself to me as Linda. "Your Grandad was a very special man, he had a wicked sense of humour and we all loved him. We are surprised that he had managed to stay with us for so long. He hadn't been eating for a while and was becoming weaker by the day. All he kept saying is that he needed to see you before he died. He made me promise that when he died, I would give you this." She hands me an envelope with the words 'Hope' written on it in Grandads handwriting. "Thank you, Linda, for looking after him in his final weeks." I put the envelope in my pocket. "Take good care now you two, and look after each other. There are plenty of people you can reach out to for support, losing someone so dear can be a shock. It will take time." These words were so familiar and took me right back to being nine years old again. "I'll leave you to say your final goodbyes."

Alice and I re-enter the room which is now silent, all the machines switched off. He peacefully lay there. We both sit looking at the man we called Grandad, the man that was treated so unfairly yet stood by our side always. I reach down to hold his hand for the final time. Memory's flood back of all the stories, fun and laughter we had over the years. What a man I had been so blessed to have known. I start crying as I realise that I would never get to talk to him or hear his voice again.

    I reach into my pocket and carefully open the envelope that Linda had given me. Inside is a hand-written note from Grandad.

Son if you're reading this then I have passed.

I need you to know how much I loved both yourself and your Dad.

I felt something wasn't right and listened to my gut for a change. I took a stash of the treasure, enough for you and Mum to have a better life. It's in the original box on your Dads boat.

Look after your Mum always.

Remember I love you so very much.

Marry Alice!

Love your Grandad

About the Author

Dealing with dyslexia has been a struggle that I've faced all my life. At school during the nineteen-eighties, dyslexia was not understood and I didn't fit into the normal way of working. It was all so very frustrating, leaving me angry and feeling so alone.

In my working life, dyslexia has slowed me down and forced me to become very disciplined with my time. Trying so hard not to fall behind on workloads and deadlines. The simplest of tasks, such as reading an email, can take ages. Writing is difficult as more often than not I can't read what I've written. Spelling leaves me frustrated as I'm forever having to check if the words are spelt right or find alternative words which I can spell or just keep my fingers crossed. This is all slow going. If I'm tired or stressed, then everything just becomes so much harder.

Technology has made such amazing progress in supporting our dyslexic community. But even now in my fifty's my dyslexia still haunts me, leaving me frustrated and often exhausted. Being dyslexic presents so many challenges that are individual. However, on the flip side, having a dyslexic brain allows me to explore my creativity and see things differently. This has been a strength that I have come to recognise and appreciate.

Exploring my creativity has been exciting and has led to many different projects. One project was developing a story based in the beautiful county of Cornwall. Spending time watching people, looking at the environment, and the way of life fuelled my imagination. Characters grew until one day The Story of Hope was born. So now what happens, what do I do with this story that's now stored in my mind? Then a moment of madness took hold when I suddenly thought I would write a book. For months I wrestled with this idea and whether it was at all achievable. I've not even read a book from start to finish let alone write one. I guess nobody knows what they can do until they try. Little did I know the extent of the challenge ahead of me.

Two years later, with hundreds and hundreds of hours invested, The Story of Hope is complete. I became addicted with every spare moment dedicated to the book in one way or another. I skipped nights out, I made excuses, I stayed up until the early hours and often was up writing at stupid o'clock in the morning. Despite my determination to see it through, once I'd started writing I soon realised I needed help. I had no idea on all the core elements required to writing a story. Sentence structure, paragraphs, past tense, present tense, I didn't know there was a thing called simile and metaphor and where to add speech marks, the list went on.

Thank you for all the amazing people that supported me. I truly could not have done this without you.

This book has not been professionally edited so be prepared to find some mistakes. I wanted my work to be true to me.

Writing this book hasn't fixed my dyslexia, it can't

be fixed. I still don't know how to spell, it still takes ages to read and even then, I don't really know what I've read.

This journey was about determination and trying to promote that if you want to have a go at something then you should, because until you try you just don't know what you can achieve. I can't believe I've managed to write a book.

Life is about having these experiences that feed your soul. Remember anything worth doing, any challenge you set yourself, will test you. It will require determination, and resilience. But that's where you get your growth, that's where you find your strength. Dream big!

Printed in Dunstable, United Kingdom